Ancient Wisdom
Sarah Lewin © 2024

Ancient Wisdom

First paperback edition March 2024

ISBN 978-0-6458504-5-1 (paperback)

ISBN 978-0-6458504-4-4 (ebook)

www.sarahlewin.com[1]

---

1. http://www.sarahlewin.com

This book is dedicated to:
My four beautiful children
My amazingly patient husband
And my friends who I have met along my journey

Where Am I?

S tella

As Stella slowly opened her eyes, she knew something was very wrong. The stench of rotten food was overpowering, mingled with the smell of hot cooking oil and petrol. The queasy feeling in the back of her throat, indicated the need to expel any remaining food lingering in her stomach. Stella didn't like strong smells, loud noises, or large quantities of stimulation of any kind. She learnt, as an adult, that these idiosyncrasies probably indicated she was somewhere on the autism spectrum. Her ears popped, the yelling and thundering of rubber tyres on the concrete road jarred her to her senses. She blinked as her eyes became accustomed to the day light. Her back felt the brick wall she was propped up against.

Why was she sitting against a wall in an alley way? There were bins on her right, and a main road on the left. Cautiously stretching her body, checking for any aches. Not feeling any pain, she stood up. The alley appeared to come to a dead end just a few metres away on her right. Stella headed towards the traffic.

Stella's memory was fuzzy. Why was she here, in a city with traffic, crowds and lots of buildings? All the things about modern life that she hated. Trying to work out the last thing she remembered. It was like trying to climb uphill in the dark, through fog.

Nothing looked familiar.

This kind of thing had happened before. Less than a year ago, Stella had found herself in a tavern in seventeenth century Scotland. Quite a shock, accidentally wandering through a portal in the bottom of her garden. Then there was the time she had found herself in the middle of a forest watching three witches chanting incantations around a fire. A witch's coven. Neither of those strange experiences, felt as unsettling as waking up in this alley. On those occasions travelling through time, she had instantly felt at home. The immediate connection with medieval Scotland was like finding long lost family and old friends.

This time, Stella felt prickly, and out of sorts. The hairs on her arms stood up and her brain felt gooey, like trying to wade through soup with gumboots on. The noises jarring with a pitch that drilled straight through every bone in her body. Dry retching, as the stench of bins and traffic fumes overwhelmed her.

"Focus on something familiar," she told herself.

The brick walls in the alley way, the grey metal of the rubbish bins and the types of cars driving past. These items familiar in the sense that she recognised she was somewhere in Australia. Stella tried to remember what state had white number plates with reddish coloured writing.

Was she in Queensland? Which part of Queensland? More importantly, why was she is Queensland and not at home?

Walking along the footpath, she read the shop signs, looking for clues. A newsagent, a laundrette, a few second-hand shops, restaurants and a women's gym. None of the shop fronts provided a clue as to her location. She caught a glimpse of her reflection in the window of the gym. Her long brown hair with a peppering of grey needed a brush. She pulled out her hair tie, ran her fingers through her hair, and tied her hair back into a messy bun.

The smell of freshly made coffee drew Stella into the first open café she came across. Her stomach constricted, sending shooting hunger pains across her body as she crossed the threshold of *The Friendly Cup*. Trying to recall her last meal made her head throb. Breathing slowly, calming herself as she waited for her order, she debated whether to ask the barista where she was, but decided against it. A quick glance at the community noticeboard, advertising for several concerts, sporting events and lost dogs confirmed she was in Brisbane.

"Are you looking for something in particular?" the smiling barista asked, handing Stella her large mocha. A little older than her, not much taller, clean shaven, with a thick mop of dark curly hair.

"Not really. I'm just checking out what is available, job vacancies, or maybe rooms to let," Stella ad-libbed. From past experiences, following her intuition provided huge benefits. Until she worked out what was happening, the café felt safe and friendly. It might be a good idea to stick around and get her bearings.

"You've come to the right place. I'm Baz, and I think we are looking for a waitress. My boss will be here soon. If you want to take a seat and wait for her, she'll probably know of any local rentals too." The barista smiled and shrugged. "If you're looking for a job in a café that is."

TAKING OFF HER LONG purple coat while she waited for Baz's boss, Stella sat at the booth nearest the front door. Since the coat had come into her possession a year ago, when she found it in the back of the cupboard of the property she was renting, it always manifested exactly what she needed at any given time. She checked the pockets and took inventory.

"Mobile phone, wallet, money—that's good, I'll count it later. Not here. Wait, what's this piece of paper?" Stella realised she was quietly speaking aloud and quickly looked around to make sure no one was paying her any attention.

33 Main Street, 2701 13:30

The piece of paper looked like it was torn from an old notepad. There were no distinguishing markings. She didn't recognise the pencil written note. As a steady stream of people poured into the café, Stella tucked everything away in her pockets. She would work it out later when she was alone.

The coffee was clearing away some of the brain fog. Stella took another sip.

She remembered taking her daughters, Andie and Emily, to the airport for their overseas adventure. Promising to visit them once they got settled into their jobs. Smiling as she recalled the start of her adventure. With her girls away for a few months, Stella had decided to spend time with her friends in seventeenth century Scotland. Through the portal in her back garden, she found kindred spirits in Brigid and Maisie. They shared a history entwined with magic. Everything easily fell into place. Able to take leave from her job, she rented her home and travelled back in time to learn more about the land that she felt an instant connection to.

In medieval Scotland there was so much to learn. Brigid owned a tavern, Maisie a dress shop, and Stella had discovered a cute little shop she was using as an apothecary. The garden out the back allowed her to grow a large selection of the herbs. Selling fresh and dried herbs to customers at the shop and the local markets. Travellers bought the more exotic remedies and potions to the market days. Stella had quickly built strong relationships with her customers and loved helping them with their herbal remedies. She rubbed her forehead, her head aching as she tried to recollect more details.

A tall, slim woman with long black hair, wearing a well-made tailored pants suit, joined her at the table. "Hello, I'm Mae. Baz tells me you might be looking for a job, and maybe somewhere to stay?"

"Stella," she said, smiling at the woman sitting across from her. "Yes, I'm looking for a job and a place to rent. For a few weeks. I am travelling around Australia." Stella was amazed at how easily she could stretch the truth. One of the advantages of her newfound gift was the ability to quickly assess the situation and react accordingly. Not that she was comfortable lying. Mae and Baz seemed genuine, but she was cautious, with no idea who she could trust.

"As it happens, we do have a vacancy for a waitress. I can only offer casual work. The hours are flexible, but ideally if you could work from about seven in the morning until four in the afternoon. Six days a week. For as long as you want to stay. How does that suit what you are looking for?" Mae asked.

"That does sound good. I do have one appointment, on Wednesday afternoon this week. I'll confirm the time as soon as I can. I don't have anything else booked." Stella paused. "I'm not sure how long I will be here either," she added.

"Wednesday afternoon won't be a problem at all." Mae smiled. "Baz mentioned that you were also looking for somewhere to stay. The flat upstairs is empty. We do have a tenant booked, but they won't need the flat until after Easter. We're going to be fixing it up, painting and repairing some minor issues. The flat has all the basics, a bed, some kitchen appliances, and furniture. The flat's yours in the meantime if you'd like it. We wouldn't charge anything, you'd be doing us a favour, having someone there while we fix it up," Mae spoke quickly, as if she was already working out what was next on her list of things to do.

"That's an awesome offer Mae. I'd love to take you up on your offer of work, and the flat upstairs sounds perfect. Thank you so much." Stella stood and smiled at Mae. "I guess I'd better start waitressing."

Setting intentions for a positive outcome. When making my morning cup of tea or coffee, take the time to think about how I want the day to pan out. Visualise and manifest only positive outcomes in every situation. Throughout the day, remember to stay positive. I can influence my life. This is magic.

The Fairy

Broomhilda

Broomhilda was in the fairy glen with the heads of the fairy folk, sprites, elves, and others who held a seat on the Council of the Realms. The Council was representative of each of the highest magical families across the realms. Stella had been instrumental in setting up this council, to combat the dangers they were facing when surges of magic were felt across the realms. The magic surges resulted in an increase in magical abilities in people like Stella. Portals opened between worlds, crossing time and space. Travel for magic folk became easier. There were fears that someone would use the increased magical energies for the wrong reasons. The council had committed to keeping an eye out across the realms for any more anomalies in magic.

"We haven't seen or heard from Stella for a few days now. We have no idea where she is." Maisie told the gathering. "It is very unusual for her not to pop in at the tavern for her morning coffee. Brigid makes the brew especially for Stella. Not many others here have acquired the taste for the bitter coffee beans. Three days ago, Stella left the tavern to help a traveller. We expected her back for tea after the tavern shut. When she missed breakfast as well, we went looking for her. She isn't in her apothecary, and she hasn't been in her room." Maisie, took a deep breath, calming herself.

Broomhilda observed Stella's friend. Maisie had the tendency to worry. "I understand you and Brigid are concerned. Probably feel responsible, for you encouraged Stella to live in our realm. It is time to stay clear headed and focused. We will find Stella. Try not to focus on what could have happened. We need to uncover the truth."

Maisie nodded. Broomhilda was worried too, but she knew better than to project her emotions onto others.

"We are attempting to locate the travellers who asked for Stella's help. It is like they never existed. Brigid is asking everyone who enters the tavern if they have seen Stella or the travellers. The travellers had a very distinct wagon, with two white horses. The wagon looked like one of those the catcher's use—for catching animals, or people." Maisie shuddered.

Looking around at the council as Maisie was talking, Broomhilda was hoping the description would jog someone's memory. The fairies were flitting around, releasing their nervous energy, the elves were talking amongst themselves, and the sprites were dancing around impatient as ever. Broomhilda took a breath, pulling herself up to her full height, of just over twenty centimetres. "We don't know if these travellers are a threat or not," she said sternly. "But we need to find Stella. The least we can do is listen to Maisie, keep an eye out for Stella, and report back any unusual occurrences."

Maisie smiled gratefully at Broomhilda. "The couple were old, with the wisdom of the ancients, and secretive. Cyril and Cleo, they said their names were. There was something odd about them. We told Stella about our concerns, but she wasn't worried. I wish we had been sterner with her. If we had accompanied her when she met them, she would be here with us now. She sees all sorts of strangers, by herself." Maisie bit her lip, determined not to cry. "We should have tried harder to keep her safe. She is a powerful witch, without understanding the full extent of her powers. Humble though."

"Stella knows how to use her magic and will use it, when it is necessary." Broomhilda reassured Maisie.

Maisie nodded. "As soon as she moved over here, she started helping others. She taught about using herbs, as if she had been doing so for years. She has this innate ability to fit in. In any situation. Remember when she jumped right in and helped us last year, when we needed someone to help close the portals?" Maisie reminded the council.

"Have you or Brigid tried to contact her through dreams?" Broomhilda asked.

One of the gifts the three women shared was the ability to spend time together in their dreams, in addition to the portal that had led Stella to the alley outside Brigid's tavern. They developed a strong bond, often spending time together through their dreams. They passed messages and warned each other of dangers, as well as practising magic skills.

"After Brigid and I had searched everywhere and couldn't find her, we were worried. We tried to contact her through our dreams. This is the first time since we have known her that we couldn't get through to her. We only called this gathering because we didn't know what else to do. We wanted to know if you have seen her or heard of any unusual occurrences," Maisie replied.

BROOMHILDA WAS A FAIRY. A normal sized fairy. Anyone who made the mistake of thinking her size meant that Broomhilda was not powerful would soon discover the extent of her magic. She was arguably one of the most powerful beings in all the realms, from one the oldest fairy families ever known. Her knowledge of the realms and her magical skills surpassed most wizards and witches. Those who made the mistake of thinking she was little and somehow inconsequential always paid the penalty. Each of the member gathered in the fairy glen, knew better than to make the mistake of doubting her.

Years of experience had taught her to always consider her options before making decisions. When she spoke, everyone listened. "We aren't aware of any unusual occurrences. None of my sources across the realms have identified any concerns. There have been no storms or unusual weather like last year. We haven't witnessed any unusually large surges of magic. No one has seen Stella. I can't feel her energy anywhere in this realm. I have tried scrying, to locate her. I haven't been able to find her anywhere. In any realm. That in itself is very unusual. I have asked around the realms if anyone else has mysteriously vanished. So far, she is the only one. There are not many people with the magical skills and abilities Stella has developed over the last twelve months. It is too early to tell if she has been taken because of her powers. Still, let's keep an eye out for anything unusual." Broomhilda hopped up on the tallest pile of stones and waved her hands over the small lake in the middle of the glen.

"If you try scrying in any large body of water, you and Brigid may be able to see Stella. Your connection with her is far stronger than mine." Broomhilda stopped speaking as an image shimmered into focus.

Stella wearing an apron, serving coffee and cake, and chatting to customers sitting at tables in a café. Waitressing. She didn't appear to be in any immediate danger.

"Typical Stella, making friends everywhere she goes. At least she is safe," Maisie breathed in relief. "Do we know exactly where she is, or why she is there, and why she hasn't tried to come back? Or maybe she has tried, and she can't make it, for some reason?"

"I can see the same thing you can, Maisie," Broomhilda said gently. "I know you are worried about your friend, but she looks like she is safe for now. As to why she is there, how she got there, or why she hasn't come back, or at least tried to contact you, I don't know yet. What I can tell, is that she is probably having trouble remembering the last few days. Her magic imprint is hazy. Now that we know where she is, we can keep an eye on her. If she doesn't try to make contact in the next couple of days, we can probably go to her and find out what is going on."

"Why do we have to wait? Why can't we go in now and bring her home?" Maisie asked Broomhilda.

"It is just a hunch I have. Now that we can see her, I can send someone to watch over her, so we don't lose her again." Broomhilda put her hand gently on Maisie's arm. "We will do our best to make sure no harm comes to her."

"Thank you. We will keep trying to make contact and will let you know if we hear from her." Maisie said. Broomhilda watched as Maisie walked quickly back into town. She would be keen to update Brigid that Stella had been located.

"I know you are keen to get back your lives, but remember Stella is one of us now. If someone has sent her away, we should all be wary, in case this is the start of some new malevolent mischief." The council members paid attention. Broomhilda's tone revealed how concerned she was. "Just keep an eye out for anything odd. Look after loved ones. I will keep you updated." With a flutter and a flurry of wings, a scurrying of feet and a lot of chattering, the elves, fairies, and sprites left the fairy glen. Everyone promised to be on the lookout for Stella and those travellers. With a sinking feeling in the pit of her stomach, Broomhilda steeled herself for the magical roller-coaster that she could sense was just around the corner.

Instead of worrying about things I cannot control, I will instead believe that everything will work out in the end. I light a candle. I write on a bay leaf, a key word to prompt the outcome I desire. Prosperity, safety, love, communication, health. I carry the leaf with me as a constant reminder that I am safe, loved and that everything will work out for the best, as it is meant to happen. This is magic.

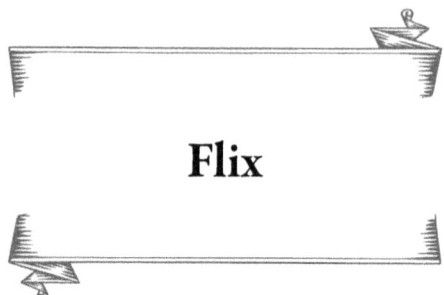

Flix

S tella

Stella appreciated being busy. Serving customers distracted her from worrying about her current situation. She would follow her intuition, stay calm, and not try to contact Brigid or Maisie.

"There is so much I want to know about why I am here, but my gut is telling me to wait," Stella whispered to herself as she wiped down the tables after lunch. The more she tried to remember, the hazier her memory. She sensed her children were safe, and that her friends across the realm weren't in any immediate danger. She focused on waitressing and chatting to customers, trusting that she would figure out the answers soon.

It was after four in the afternoon when Stella hung up her apron and collected her coat.

"Any chance of another coffee before I go?" she asked Baz. "Unless you've turned off the machine already."

"Of course for you, Stella!" He beamed. 'You've earned it. A hit with the customers today! It doesn't take long to wipe the coffee machine. There's some left-over peppermint slice if you're interested," he added, pointing to a container on the bench. "Mae left the key for the flat, in the drawer under the cash register. When you go out the back door, up the back stairs and you can't miss the flat." Baz handed Stella her coffee and a bag with a generous piece of peppermint slice. "I'll see you bright and early tomorrow."

SITTING AT THE DINING table with her coffee and slice, Stella appreciated the peace and quiet after a day of chatting and the noise of the café. Savouring the taste of coffee, and the chocolate and peppermint slice, the knot of tension in her neck and across the top of her head started to ease. The migraine still lurked around the edges, around her eyes. Refusing to let the pain interfere with what she was doing, she whispered "I am not getting a migraine."

Emptying her pockets, placing her phone and wallet to one side, Stella read the words on the piece of paper.

33 Main Street, 2701 13:30

She hadn't noticed the tiny symbol on the bottom of the note before. The infinity symbol inside a circle, drawn faintly in pencil. She recognised it as a sigil from Brigid and Maisie's *Book of Spells*. They were showing her how to create her own book. A witchy book to keep track of recipes, rituals, and ideas for celebrating the yearly festivals, or the phases of the moon. She remembered adding drawing of herbs and diagrams. Soon she would learn the significance of sigils, the symbols that formed part of a witch's spell casting, incantations, and ritual.

The map on her mobile confirmed 33 Main Street wasn't far from the café. She could easily walk there. The calendar app indicated it was Monday 25 of January. If 2701 was the date and 13:30 was the time; then something important was happening at 33 Main Street in two days. Energy tingled and bounced through Stella's body, partly due to the coffee and the chocolate, and partly at the thought of what she might discover on Wednesday. Joining her hands together, fingertips touching, slow and steady breaths to calm the energy bouncing around every cell of her body. One of the first signs of her magic was uncontrollable energy. Whenever she was emotional, agitated, upset or angry, her energy manifested itself in sparks of energy. Electrical appliances would malfunction. Though her brain was foggy, she instinctively knew to minimise her use of magic.

Suddenly exhausted, Stella lay down on the bed. "Just for five minutes. There is so much more I want to figure out," she murmured, drifting off to sleep.

FROM HIS POSITION ON the windowsill, the sprite, Flix, watched over Stella as she slept.

In her dreams, Stella danced around the bonfire with Maisie and Brigid as she had many times before. This time was different. No matter how loudly she called, she couldn't make them hear. In the flat, tossing and turning in her sleep she tried to get their attention.

Broomhilda's direction to the sprite was to watch over Stella and keep her safe. Flix scanned the room as she slept.

"At least while you are asleep you should be safe," he whispered softly to Stella. Turning his attention to the car park below, he saw a hooded figure. Trying to hide, crouched under the gum tree in the darkest corner of the empty space. Flix watched the mysterious figure as she muttered to herself, watching Stella's window, weaving a ball of fog with her hands.

STELLA AWOKE TO DARKNESS. No moonlight shone through the window. On the eve of the new moon, the world was plunged into darkness. Objects were hidden—mysterious—not as they seem. She knew it as a time of planning new adventures and projects. Knowing what was important and releasing what was no longer needed. The growth of plants, the ocean tides, animals and human emotions linked to the phases of the moon. Before she travelled to the other realm, she had an interest in nature, seasons and phases of the moon.

A wave of nausea swept over her, as she remembered where she was. Not certain how long she had slept, her mind raced. It was tough not knowing the motive behind her arrival back into her timeline. Her stomach gurgled, her head pounded, and her muscles ached. She consoled herself that she would soon be reunited with her coven. Stretching, as the familiar tingling of her power returned. Hoping her memory would follow, she forced herself to stay positive. To set intentions and live in the present moment were skills she learnt as a mum. Stella suspected these tools might come in handy in her current situation. Her bottom lip pulsed as she bit it. She was tempted to message her girls, Andie and Emily. Her instinct told her to wait; they were safe. If anything were wrong, one of them would contact her.

Sitting cross-legged on the bed, Stella remembered when she first discovered her magical abilities. With her hands held in front of her body, she visualised a golden ball of energy forming between her palms. Moving her hands in a rhythm she sensed in her body, she manipulated the ball as it grew and pulsed. From the tiniest orb of light, the sphere grew until it filled her hands. Stella lifted her hands above her head as the energy pulsated in her palms. Balancing it firmly, she pushed the ball of light through the crown of her head.

As the golden orb vibrated throughout her body, Stella's memory returned. She inhaled sharply. Her heart racing, she quickly glanced around to ensure she was alone. She scanned for a concealed portal, or a way to communicate with her coven. Instinct told her to proceed cautiously.

FLIX

Flix watched Stella control her energy. He didn't leave to alert Broomhilda when Stella's memory returned. He was in no doubt of his role—stay with Stella, protect her, keep her safe. Ascertain if she was in any danger, inform Broomhilda of any significant developments, but do not leave Stella alone. He opened and closed his tiny hands, to steady his energy and keep balance on the windowsill. While he didn't possess nerves of steel, the sprite was patient. He ignored his stomach which felt like it contained thousands of ants marching in circles.

Sensing he was not the only person interested in what was happening in the flat, he scanned the car park. The hooded figure was still hiding in the shadows. Flix possessed the ability to feel the energy and auras of other creatures. The dizziness that he felt, as he split his focus between Stella and the unknown being outside, was familiar. Flix wiggled his fingers, balancing his senses, a trick he learnt years ago. He had been on plenty of similar missions.

KAI

The hooded figure in the car park felt the change in energy. She moved back further into the shadow cast by the trees. She couldn't afford to be seen by anyone who may be watching out for Stella. This figure in the darkness, known by the name Kai, was a witch imprisoned, torn away from her coven for daring to stand up for others. The exile was the price she paid for protecting a group of humans who accidentally found themselves in the wrong place. She transported them to safety. Now at the mercy of those who had restrained her, forcing her to take part in this deception. Wincing as she stretched, the bruise on her leg a reminder that she couldn't escape her employers, yet.

Kai had been directed to ensure Stella didn't remember the details that led her to wake up in an alley in Brisbane. *Don't make contact. Don't interfere.* Her orders were clear. *Observe and report. If compromised, leave quietly. Otherwise, don't leave your post.* She shivered, knowing that to disobey would mean more bruises, or worse. As she slid further back into the shadows, she focused on the light radiating from the window. Kai smiled. She had a plan to free herself from her employers. If she played her hand correctly.

STELLA

Stella tried to ignore the feeling of dread that was cramping the toes on her right foot. An old injury, back before she lost her children, it often ached during times of stress. She didn't sense there was any immediate danger to her—now grown up—children. Worrying about them was a luxury she couldn't afford in her present predicament.

She searched the kitchenette and found an old black pen and some envelopes piled in a corner of the bench. Gasping at the cold as she splashed water on her face, she a filled glass from the tap. She drained the glass and filled it again. She could feel eyes on her back as she sipped water in front of the window. She turned to scan the room. Nothing. She peered through the window to the empty street outside. Lace curtains, on either side of the window, were decorative at best.

She sat crossed legged in the middle of the bed. Without turning on the light, Stella hastily scribbled notes, jotting down everything she remembered, in case she forgot again.

The girls are safe. They landed in the UK before Christmas. The other two are safe or the girls would let me know.

I rented my home to my neighbour's mum, for six months.

Just before Christmas I moved over to Maisie and Brigid's. I am setting up my apothecary, helping a whole lot of different people. Some strangers had visited and asked for help. When I took them to my shop to show them herbs and potions, something happened. Did they knock me out? The next thing I remember is waking up in Brisbane.

What else?

Stella concentrated on her breathing, slowly calming her energy—a skill she had not yet perfected. Small electric sparks bounced around the room, eventually fading into the darkness. Rubbing her itchy eyes, and cringing at the buzzing in her ears, Stella recognised the signs. Her energy was looking for an outlet. She couldn't afford her to have her energy explode if she couldn't calm her emotions.

Over the last few months her magic and intuition grew as she learnt to trust herself. *Breathe, calm, focus.* She blinked as images flashed by, like scenes from a movie. She recalled the travellers; their names were Cleo and Cyril. Maisie and Brigid warned her not to trust them or take them to her apothecary. Ignoring her friends, Stella invited them into her store. They asked for potions to treat their insomnia. As she turned to reach for the herbs that were required, they covered her face with a cloth. Drifting into sleep she heard snippets of their conversation; *Remove her—wipe her memory—she would know what to do* …

Her heart racing, she made more notes. Why did they want her out of the way? How could she let her friends know what was happening? Logic told her there must be a portal nearby. A sudden movement on the windowsill caught her attention. Stella covered her mouth with her hands to stop the noise that was threatening to escape. She watched as a sprite tip toed towards her, holding his finger to his lips.

"Hi," he whispered. "I'm Flix. Broomhilda sent me here to look out for you. You gave us quite a scare disappearing like that." He nodded as Stella opened her mouth. "Yes, we know it wasn't your fault."

Feeling her energy building up again, she moved off her bed, sliding on the floor to be closer to her new friend. "I want to contact my friends, to tell them it was two strangers who dragged me here. I haven't remembered everything that happened. It's as if someone replaced my brain with fairy floss. No matter how hard I try to remember or contact my friends, nothing works. My intuition is telling me not to perform any kind of magic or look for a portal to try to return home yet."

"That's wise," agreed Flix. "There is someone watching you. Outside, in the shadows. I am not sure if they have seen me. They were focused on you. Your energy." A look of horror crossed Stella's face. Flix hastily added, "Don't worry. I can pass the information along to

Broomhilda and your friends. I am to stay, to make sure you are safe, for as long as you are stuck here." He patted her hand. "It is smart, not using your magic, for now. If you write a message, I will make sure it reaches your friends."

"Oh, thank you!" Stella said, scribbling on the second envelope she had found in the kitchen. *I'm safe. In my time, in Australia. Being watched. Following clues. Not safe to use magic. Will be in contact as soon as I can. Watch out for Cleo and Cyril. Dangerous. Do not trust. Stay safe x.*

Stella smiled wryly, noting that it was her friends who had initially warned Stella against trusting the travellers. She promised herself next time to pay heed to their words. Signing the note, she folded it into a tiny square and handed it to Flix.

"Thank you," she whispered again, grateful to have a way to contact her friends. It was comforting that Flix understood the magic realm.

"Not a problem," he replied. "Try to get some sleep. Stay calm, I have heard what happens when you get worked up about something." He winked.

Flix moved silently back to his window vantage point. The sprite was right. One of the first signs that she had supernatural abilities was that her anger, sadness, or frustration would cause electrical appliances to malfunction. There were also weird weather patterns that may have been partly her fault. Stella had learnt to control these events. Now, as she lay in her bed, her body buzzed with energy. Kidnapped, dragged through a portal, and trapped here. She must be careful. Heed the sprites words—the possibility of danger was real. Someone was outside observing her movements. Her instincts not to use magic were right.

She should have been more concerned about Flix's warning that someone was outside keeping an eye on her. Feeling her energy bubbling just below the surface, she realised that she wasn't scared. That feeling, the millions of tiny feathers tickling her arms and legs, she recognised now as excitement.

STELLA COULDN'T SLEEP. Used to hearing the voices of her spirit guides and ancestors as they whispered advice, it was far too quiet in her room above the cafe. She trusted in these messages as she would her own intuition. Was their silence a ploy to keep her safe, hidden from sight? She snuggled under the covers. Questions ran in circles around her brain. She could feel them as if they possessed an energy independent of her own. Why did the travellers choose her? Why move her but not harm her? Who was in danger? How could she resolve whatever the impending crisis was? Where would she find the answers? The breath caught in her throat. She had to quell the rising panic at the thought of her friends or family being in danger. She held her breath, slowing easing it out through her mouth.

Everyone made a fuss about how powerful Stella was, and how strong her magic was. She still thought of herself as Stella. Single mother of four who had made some monumental mistakes. But, seeing as she had been forcefully removed from a realm where magic and healing was commonplace, someone must have seen her as a threat. A threat to what?

The only clue so far was the note that appeared in the pocket of her favourite coat. Her captors mustn't know that the coat would manifest what she needed at just the right time. The right crystal, a specific combination of herbs, a list of ingredients or a recipe for a healing potion. The location, the date and time pointed to somewhere that might hold some answers. Encouraged by the fact her coat had never let her down, Stella decided to try and get some sleep.

When I believe in myself the magic really starts to step it up a notch. When I look in the mirror and smile at the amazing and awesome person smiling at me. I create the self-love that is so important for my mental and physical health. It is more than that. I am casting a spell, giving myself the permission to be the best version of me. To let go of the fear that is holding me back. This is magic too.

33 Main Street

Stella

The shrill beeping of the alarm on her phone jolted Stella awake. Peering at the mobile, she saw it was 6 am. She didn't remember setting her alarm. Grateful it had woken her, she closed her eyes for a few seconds, tempted to drift back into a dreamless sleep. Until she remembered where she was. Peering over to the windowsill for reassurance that the sprite was still there. Flix smiled and waved. He had propped up one end of the blinds and was sitting in the gap on his side so that he could see Stella and the car park.

Jumping out of bed, she grabbed her clothes. These would have to do. Not too smelly or dirty yet, although another day in the café would change that. She must ask Baz if there was a second-hand shop nearby. A phone charger would be handy too. Her mobile only had twenty percent battery. Checking the wardrobe to see if by chance the last tenant had left behind any clothes, Stella was pleased to find some items in a pile on the floor. The blue shirt wasn't her first choice, but it was clean, and the jeans were her size. Tapping the back of the wardrobe, on the off chance there was a hidden portal, Stella shrugged. It was worth a shot.

"COFFEE AND RAISIN TOAST." Baz smiled, handing her a plate and a cup as she opened the door. "I'm making a savoury mince that's to die for. It'll be ready in ten minutes. Unless you're vegetarian. Well, even then it will be ready in ten minutes, you just don't have to eat any."

"You're amazing Baz! I love you!" Putting her plate and cup on the bench, Stella hugged Baz, overcome with emotion at the kindness he had shown to her. Maybe everything would be okay after all. She would solve the mystery and get back to her friends. Travel overseas to spend time with her daughters.

"Oh, my goodness, I love cooking! And feeding people. It's my thing." Baz blushed. Stella wondered if he was used to receiving compliments.

"I imagine there are many people who are very happy you are passionate about cooking. Helping people is my thing too. Well, it is when I am at home." Stella reached into her pocket for her money. "Will you at least let me pay for breakfast?"

Baz shook his head, hiding his hands around his back, looking mortally wounded that she would even suggest such a thing.

"I'm not vegetarian, well, not all the time. And I love the sound of savoury mince." Stella put on her apron as she polished off the toast and coffee. Her grateful stomach reminding her that she hadn't eaten much over the last couple of days.

"I'm looking forward to today," she said to no one in particular. She missed her home, her children, and her friends. She was confident that Flix would pass her message on to them as soon as he could. "I figure the best distraction to missing home, is to get stuck in doing something productive." She smiled, the familiar buzz of energy humming along in her body, heightening her awareness of her surroundings.

Stella sensed that Baz was going to ask about her home. Why she was travelling, and who she was missing? Thankfully, the bell above the door rang, signifying the start of the morning coffee rush.

MAISIE AND BRIGID

In an alternate realm sat a tavern in Scotland back in the seventeenth century. Two women stood at the bar in the middle of the tavern. The bar owner with dark red hair was similar in age to Stella. The other woman's hair was lighter, her eyes were a dark green hue that changed depending on how she was feeling. She owned the dress shop a few doors down from the tavern. The portal that Stella stumbled through last year had led her here.

"It's just not the same without Stella," Brigid said, handing Maisie a steaming hot tankard of coffee.

"I am sure she will be back in no time," Maisie reassured Brigid. "We both know how strong she is. I don't just mean her magic. If she can find a way to get back, or to contact us, she will." Maisie drained her tankard, passing it back for a refill.

"True." Brigid handed her friend back the tankard full of coffee, laced with a little whisky. "To fortify us for the day ahead," she said, as Maisie took a sip. "I was looking forward to celebrating the dark moon with her last night." Brigid mused, absent mindedly polishing one of the tankards hanging behind the bar.

"There will be plenty of other opportunities to celebrate with her," replied Maisie. "Are you planning on cleaning the whole tavern? Because if so, I think you missed a spot over there, in the corner, where the little mouse lives." She smiled. Having been friends for as long as they could remember there was a comfortableness about their relationship. At times it felt like they were closer than sisters. Meeting Stella last year, they both immediately felt that same connection with her.

A knock at the door caught their attention, as did the small piece of paper they watched slide under the door. Opening the door, looking left and right down the alleyway, Brigid expected to see someone hurrying away. There was no one there. She didn't notice the tiny carrier fairy who flew off to her next job, having deposited Stella's note under the door.

Brigid picked up the note and together they read the words Stella had scribbled in the dark the night before. "At least she is safe." Maisie breathed a sigh of relief. "I just want to go and get her and bring her home."

"We need to tell Broomhilda about this first. If Stella is right, and she normally is, then Cleo and Cyril wanted to get her out of the way. I don't think they are working alone. If they are planning something big maybe they needed their biggest threat out of the way. We must warn

Broomhilda and the others." Brigid was already closing and locking the heavy wooden front door of the tavern, packing them some breakfast for the trip.

"I'll look after the tavern, while you are gone." The youth who had slid in through the back door, moved, startling both women.

"Thanks Oscar. Remember what I have taught you," Brigid said. 'No drinking anything off the top shelf. You can eat anything you are willing to make. Don't let anyone in. If you do your chores, we will pay you when we get back." She had a soft spot for the orphan and paid him for keeping the tavern clean. He got food and drink and a safe spot to sleep when he needed it.

STELLA

Stella assumed that the person who was watching her from the shadows, would probably come into the café at some point. At least that's what she would do. She scanned the room for anyone looking like they were trying to hide. It was the quiet time between the early morning coffee run and the lunch rush. Stella thought about it, if she was staking out a suspect, she would have called in early and returned when it was busy. She made a mental note to keep an eye out for a hooded figure, next time it got busy.

THE CAFÉ BUZZED AS many of the regulars chose their favourite booths. Others were happy to order takeaway. Mae had donned an apron and was making the drinks, while Baz busily prepared the meals, and Stella served the customers who chose to eat in. There was not a spare seat in the café. Stella picked at least three possible suspects. All wearing dark hoodies. Two were men, similar in age to Stella. Computer gamers, who rarely left the house maybe? Or did they work nights and were grabbing lunch before heading home. Both with their noses pressed close to their phone screens, shovelling chips into their mouths and paying no attention to their surroundings.

It was harder to pick the age of the female, whose face was mostly hidden. She was of slim build and wearing no make-up. As she delivered water, a coffee, and a piece of chocolate mud cake, she spoke to the lady. "This is my idea of a perfect meal!" Stella beamed innocently, attempting to make conversation. The woman smiled, making eye contact for a few seconds.

The café was full. Stella was kept busy serving, with little opportunity to keep an eye on the hooded customer. She watched the woman go, glancing at Stella before leaving the café.

"WHERE ARE YOU OFF TO this afternoon?" Baz asked as he wiped the countertop and the coffee machine. The dishes were done, and he had finished his food prep for the following day.

"I thought I'd go for a walk and check out the neighbourhood." Stella hoped she sounded more relaxed than she felt. Straightening the chairs and wiping the tables was distracting her from her current predicament.

"You're here on a holiday, is that right?" Baz asked. "I've only ever lived here, in Brisbane, and always in the same suburb. I like hearing stories about adventures from people who are brave enough to travel."

"Do you want to travel one day?" Stella asked, smiling as she remembered that up until last year, she also had lived most of her life in one place. Finding she had magical abilities changed all that. The portal that took her to another realm. Meeting her coven. Winning a competition allowing her to travel to the United Kingdom. Visiting Stonehenge. Helping to save the world from a sinister coven. Switching between realms felt perfectly normal. Her life had changed forever less than twelve months earlier.

"Maybe, although I think I prefer listening to other people's stories. I don't like change," Baz mused, polishing the chrome of the coffee machine.

"I live down south, near Canberra. I'm up here for a break, to travel and to see some more of our wonderful country. I just decided one day to hop on a bus and see where it took me. I stay in one place for a while, then I move on." Stella smiled. "Do you live close by?"

"I bus it in from a couple of suburbs away. Mae's a great boss. I love the job. Now go, have fun, see the sights. I'll finish here." He waved her away.

As she left the café, she resisted the urge to look over her shoulder. She hoped Flix was nearby. It was comforting to know he was watching out for her. Stella was curious to see what the hooded figure would do. Would she be able to identify her as the lady who ate chocolate mud cake? Would anyone else be following her?

The street was crowded with people hurrying home from work, or wherever else it was people in Brisbane travelled to in the late afternoon. It was difficult to keep her emotions and her energy in check. The last thing Stella needed was her energy exploding. She was determined to locate Main Street. Counting out her steps, pretending she was out for a casual stroll after work, rather than trying to solve a mystery.

The shopfronts looked no different to anywhere else Stella had lived. It wasn't so different to Canberra. Except Canberra was cold, and full of public servants. It had suited her while her children were small. Here there were just as many people, and lots of shops and businesses vying for customers. People hurried past each other, not stopping to chat. Each shopfront told a story. Some were old, brick original buildings from the early 1900s. Others newer and garish, with square brick facades. Jewellers, newsagents, women's clothes shops, medical centres, and accountants. Every second or third door led to a café, a hot chip shop or a Chinese takeaway.

Stella's curiosity was piqued. How did all these businesses make a living? There were so many cafes, pubs, and shops with the same old stuff in them. Unless locals shopped close to where they lived, picking up groceries between the train station and their way home. Stella cringed. She wouldn't want to rely on public transport. She shuddered. Too many people crowded and jostling. Too much noise and smells that made her gag. Rubbing her aching temples with each step. Her empath skills took its toll when she found herself in the presence of others. Being in such close proximity to many people drained her. Projecting a cloak of invisibility always helped to keep detached from the energy of others.

It was difficult to tell whether anyone was following her. Stella twirled as if she was sightseeing. The street was still crowded. The number of people in hoodies, even in summer - joggers, fitness junkies, and people who wanted to hide, to blend in. Pretending to gaze into a gift shop window she clenched her fists. No one appeared to be paying her any attention. She couldn't dawdle too long at any one place. It was safer to keep moving. She figured it was harder to be kidnapped if she stayed with the crowd.

Stella turned into Main Street. She dodged people hurrying past, pulling her coat tightly around herself. It was summer but once the sun sank behind the buildings, there was a real chill to the air.

SHE WAS PROUD OF THE fire-pit she built in the front garden of her cottage. An open fire was soothing. In the absence of her firepit, her purple coat was warm enough. Stella couldn't wait to solve the mystery and return home to her cottage. To return to the other realm and spend time with her friends. To learn more about her magic abilities. Overcoming obstacles was becoming all too frequent for Stella's liking. She hadn't survived single parenthood unscathed. Her determination to one day be reunited with her children propelled her forward each day. Discovering that magic came at a price hadn't phased her.

The revelation that she had magic powers had changed her life. Her abilities did make a difference, but there was so much more that Stella was grateful for. Time spent with two of her daughters. The opportunity to travel the world, and to travel between the realms. Connections with people who mattered.

Not sure if she was being followed, she continued along Main Street. Instinctively she turned into the next shop. Opening the door to the newsagents, she watched the lady who ate mud cake for lunch cross the road. Pretending to browse the magazines she observed the lady walk into laundrette. A minute or so later, the lady exited the building and glanced towards the newsagent. As Stella flicked through a magazine on organic gardening the woman disappeared back towards the café.

"I highly recommend those magazines, if you are an avid gardener." A man whose shirt identified him as Peter K joined Stella at the magazine rack. He was similar in age to her son. He was friendly, and she was reminded of her son. When he was small and before the family curse tore them apart.

"I'm here on holidays," Stella responded. There was no time for reminiscing. Focus on the present. "I am missing my garden though. I have a subscription to this one at home." She did buy the local paper, assuming that it may contain some useful information. Stella headed back toward the café. It had not escaped her attention that the laundrette was located at 33 Main Street.

Research, investigation and preparation are important to me. I spend time finding the information I need before I take action. I am prepared for every option and opportunity that comes my way. Checking facts and information and being prepared is casting a spell. This is magic.

Across the Realms

Brigid and Maisie

"We shouldn't be surprised that Broomhilda knew we were coming, even before we called her." Brigid nodded her agreement with Maisie's statement as they knocked on the door of Broomhilda's castle. The dilapidated ancient building was a façade behind which Broomhilda, and her family had lived for centuries. Fairy magic was unique. The veil had been woven across the castle exterior, an enchantment that only fairies could create. What looked like castle ruins to humans and other beings, hid the complex world of the fae. Those who could see beyond the veil, witnessed a whole other world. Hundreds of fairies and thousands of species of flowers and plants known only to the magic folk. The base of an ancient magic allowing communication through the complex fae network. Broomhilda oversaw it all.

"I am pleased to hear that Stella has been found and she is safe. It is disturbing that there is a sinister element in our realm. We have Flix watching out for her. She isn't in any danger. We still don't know why she was taken. I am more concerned about whether our realm is going to be targeted."

"Brigid and I were being a little melodramatic. Maybe whoever took Stella was planning something sinister here. They didn't want Stella in our realm because she might be able to stop it. I am sure that is just us jumping to conclusions and that there isn't really any danger," Maisie said hopefully.

'I fear you are probably right, that we have an element in the realm who wanted Stella out of the way for some reason," Broomhilda mused. "We need to work out what they are planning, so we can work out if we need to bring her back here, or whether she needs to stay in her realm. There are benefits to both. She has such raw power, which is still so untapped and unknown. There is no point doing anything until we know a little more about what is actually going on." Broomhilda paused, watching a group of fairies dropping seeds into a freshly dug garden bed.

"Did you know we grow many of the herbs used in aromatherapy? Most of them were created in this realm. We plant by the phases of the moon, taking into consideration the changing weather of the seasons. The lavender over there will be ready for harvest in less than six months. We have the best soil in the realm. The peppermint we planted last dark moon has already been harvested to make teas." Broomhilda waved her arms and half a dozen fairies at the end of the seeding line broke off, flying away to the left, disappearing behind the bee hives. "Honey." Broomhilda nodded. "We are little, but never underestimate the power and strength of a fairy."

"I don't think we should underestimate Stella either," Brigid added, steering the conversation back to the problem at hand.

"Yes," Broomhilda agreed. "Before we make any decisions about Stella, we need to figure out who the travellers really are, why they moved Stella out of the way, and what they have planned. Last night, the dark moon, would have been the perfect opportunity to start something. I haven't felt any surge or inkling that there is a disturbance in this realm. I have sent my scouts out into the other realms to check for any anomalies."

"What can we do to help?" Brigid asked.

"My sources will report back to me by the end of the nights new moon. Our realm and Stella's are likely the source of the trouble. More magical humans live across these worlds than in the other realms. Humans' impatience and greed, their need for power and control are often the cause of many issues." Broomhilda paused, "Have you spoken to Luna and the others? They have contacts throughout the realms."

Luna, Catherine and Tizzie, were older and with more contacts throughout the lands where magic was commonplace. Luna, like Stella, chose to render assistance in this realm many years ago. She lost her family as a result. Luna wore her long dark hair up in a bun. Catherine's blonde hair fell around her shoulders. Tizzie's curly red hair stood out in a crowd. Strong women. The six women had formed a bond.

"We spoke to Luna yesterday. We will join them this evening to celebrate the new moon. We will know more then," Brigid responded. The witches were different in many ways, but there were uncanny similarities. Catherine, like Brigid, owned and ran a tavern in medieval Scotland. Tizzie and Maisie both owned dress shops and Luna, like Stella, owned an apothecary and helped people with a range of ailments. Both covens worked well together and were just as powerful separately. Their combined experience was a force that not many people would be foolish enough to challenge. Yet someone did. Stella was removed from her coven, and it was seeming more likely that their combined power had something to do with it.

"We need to know if there have been any sightings of unusually large gatherings. Also, have there been more travellers than normal? If there is a coven trying to cause trouble, they must be organised, and it is likely they are large in numbers. We are looking for people who are not happy with their lives. Those who talk about wanting more power. Groups that incite others, encouraging unruly behaviour." Broomhilda confirmed Brigid's concerns.

A group of fairies flew overhead, following some butterflies and bees as they weaved in amongst the flowers. "I must go now. I will send someone to the tavern at first light tomorrow. We will consolidate our information and work out what the next steps are. Be assured that we will continue to keep an eye on Stella. No harm will come to her."

Maisie and Brigid watched as Broomhilda flew away. "We will reach more people if we work in different teams," Maisie suggested as they walked briskly back to town. "Logan will meet us at the tavern after his coven checks the other side of town. They were happy to help when we needed to close the portals. I know they will be keen to help us find Stella. I will gather the other women from our circle. Ask them to reach out to their groups. You can stay in the tavern and check with everyone who comes in. I was even thinking of offering a reward for anyone who has any information."

"That's a good idea," agreed Brigid. "Luna might have news when we see her tonight." As they approached the edge of town, several groups of people hurried past them, on the way out of town. Normally this was the time of day when people came into the town; to sell their wares, look for work, or buy food and supplies. It was unusual to see people leaving town this early in the day.

Maisie saw one of her customers hurrying past. She tapped her on the arm, startling her, "Excuse me, Harriet? What is happening? Why are so many people leaving town?"

"Um, hi Maisie, I can't stop. You should probably turn around and leave too." She nodded nervously at Brigid.

"Why?" Maisie held Harriet's arm. Several more people struggled past them on the road, carrying bundles of clothes and food on their backs. "What's going on?"

"Honestly, I don't really know. Someone came running through the streets telling us there was danger and to leave now." Harriet looked around nervously. "I swear I don't know why, but most of the people in the street left straight away."

"THANKS HARRIET, STAY safe." Maisie let go of her arm, watching her hurry down the road.

"What do you make of that?" Maisie asked Brigid.

"I don't know but if I was planning something underhanded, it is smart to scare nearly everyone away. Makes it easier to control who is left." Brigid shrugged. "But if this is what is happening, it's likely that those who stay behind are braver, less scared, and more difficult to control. It could be an interesting week."

"I'll be back after lunch." Maisie hugged Brigid at the tavern door.

"We will be okay. Stella will be okay," Brigid whispered. Maisie hurried to her shop. She waved back at Brigid, hoping that was true.

STELLA

The walk in the cool afternoon air had cleared out some of the cobwebs tangled around Stella's brain. Her nerves tingled in her head, a million tiny pins and needles. The mist cleared, lifting the veil that had draped over her since she woke up in the alleyway.

Spying a convenience store on the way back to the flat, she made a detour. She hoped to find some items of clothing, a phone charger, and maybe some snacks. Stella opened the door and was blasted with a sudden icy blast of air conditioning and deafening music. For twenty dollars she purchased a notepad and pen, underwear, socks, strawberries, and some chocolate. She was willing to put up with the noise and the temperature drop to buy what she needed, at a reasonable price. The hot air as she re-entered the street, she was prepared for, enveloped her in an unwelcome, sweaty hug.

Sitting on her doorstep was a box containing some coffee sachets, a carton of milk, two salad sandwiches and a note *I hope you enjoyed your walk, Baz.* What a nice man. He reminded Stella of her favourite uncle. She had paid attention in the café. Baz chatted with all the customers, remembering their names and other details. He must love his job, and his customers.

She set the box on the bench in the kitchen. Her neck muscle loosened as she put the food in the coffee sachets in the cupboard. Moving her arm up and down as the pain eased, she could move her head more freely than before. Once the strawberries, chocolate, milk, and sandwiches were in the fridge, she sighed. This wasn't home. She wasn't planning on staying long but it was satisfying to put things away. in their place. She put the underwear and socks away in the wardrobe.

Back in the kitchen, she made herself a coffee. She carried her mug to the table, savouring the aroma. The smell of coffee was familiar and comforting. Stella sat down with the notebook. Taking control of the situation was also comforting. She wrote the date, and then the information from the note she had found. Tomorrow was the date identified on the note; 2701. 33 Main Street was the laundrette. She knew where and when, just not what she would find when she arrived. At least she would have an opportunity to wash her clothes. She made a mental note to ask Baz if there was an op shop nearby. She didn't remember seeing one during her walk.

"Excuse me." Flix walked over from his position on the windowsill. In one fluid movement, he jumped up and landed on the spare chair next to her. "How was your walk this afternoon?"

"I was trying to see if I was being followed. I also needed to find 33 Main Street." Stella gently lifted Flix up, so he was sitting on the table, noticing his clothes for the first time. The sprite was dressed in a long-sleeved black top and blue jeans. With tiny little work boots. She was curious as to why he was dressed this way, but she thought it impolite to ask.

"It is easier to blend in wearing clothes similar to the world where we are working. If we are noticed, people they aren't as surprised as you would think. Their brain disregards small beings dressed normally. If we wore sparkles or wings it would attract more attention." Flix responded to her mental query. "Yes, I can read your mind to a degree. I hear your questions before you ask them. You were being followed, but I think you know that. 33 Main Street. May I ask how do you know about that building? Why are you interested in it?"

Curious at the way Flix asked the question, Stella countered, "What do you know about that?"

"Legend is that 33 Main Street is where magic folk gather. Covens celebrate the harvests in the park behind the laundrette. There is a portal in the building somewhere. Not a place I would recommend going into while you are trying to hide. It could be dangerous." The sprite stretched his arms and stood up, trying to look stern and imposing. Stella chuckled.

"I have a coat that found me when I first discovered my magical abilities. The pockets are always gifting me with presents, a crystal, a pouch of herbs, pieces of paper, a key. Whatever I find in the pockets is normally exactly what I need at that time. Yesterday my coat gave me this piece of paper. The address 33 Main Street was written on it. With a date and time, tomorrow afternoon. I think it means I am meant to be there at the laundrette, at that time." Seeing the look on the sprite's face, she added, "I'll be careful."

"The hooded figure who followed you; her name is Kai. You saw her enter and leave the laundrette. She wasn't in there for long. I stayed near you, so I don't know what she was up to." Flix shook his finger at her in mock sternness. "I understand that I am not going to be able to stop you going tomorrow. I have been advised you can handle yourself. Broomhilda did suggest you gather information, rather than act."

Stella nodded. Hearing the head fairy's name provided comfort. "Do Brigid and Maisie know I am okay?"

"Yes. They are working with Broomhilda on the theory that you were sent here, away from their realm. Likely because someone is planning something and needed you out of the way. But don't be worried about them," Flix added. "Broomhilda is almost as old as magic itself. Brigid and Maisie can protect themselves too."

"Do they know when it will be safe for me to go back home?"

"Not yet. They want to learn more about what is going on. I know that isn't the answer you wanted to hear." Flix leaned in, as if to comfort her. She appreciated the gesture, but she wasn't sure if trying to hug the sprite would injure him.

"Can I get another message to them? After I go to Main Street tomorrow?" Stella asked. "I hope to have more information then."

"Yes. I can get the information across to them." Flix hopped back onto the floor. "You should try to get some sleep. I'll keep a look out."

Stella lay on the bed. She knew performing magic was dangerous. She took a deep breath in. As she exhaled, she pictured her invisibility cloak covering her. She sensed its velvety cloth enveloping her and keeping her safe. She closed her eyes. Letting images flow she viewed the scenes flashing past her consciousness. Like stills from a movie. Brigid was in the bar, talking to customers, as she passed them tankards of ale. Maisie was chatting with some women, poring over hand drawn maps. The tavern window behind her friend drew her gaze. The sky was deep purple. Could it be the Northern lights? She heard the gasps and chatter of people, but she couldn't make out any words. The more she concentrated on trying to hear what they were saying, the more the voices faded.

Stella got out of bed and stretched. Instinctively she knew not to force the images. She moved quietly around the room. Pacing slowly, looking for hidden objects. If there was a portal or any other evidence of magic it was well masked. She took her coat from the chair where she had dumped it after her afternoon's expedition and checked the pockets. She smiled. Tucked in the bottom of one of the pockets was a moonstone. Small enough to fit in the palm of her hand.

She cupped the stone; its coolness was soothing. It was the first night of the new moon. Stella sat on the pillows on the bed and placed the stone on her forehead. Images flooded in. Under a purple and red sky, groups of people stood gathered in long robes, like the robes she wore with her coven, but darker. A sinister feeling, dark and foreboding descended as she squinted to see more details. Their faces were blurred. The image started to fade.

Pocketing the stone, she stood up. Outside, under the new moon, she saw the hooded figure crouched under the tall eucalypt in the corner. Keeping an eye on the figure, she whispered to Flix, sharing the images she had seen. "There were twelve hooded figures, or maybe thirteen. Gathered in a clearing. Can you pass this onto Broomhilda, so she can make the necessary preparations? I think it was on the edge of town. Not near the forest. Close to where we met for the bonfire." She realised she knew more than she thought.

"No wonder they sent you away," Flix said in awe. "If you could see that much from here, without using magic, I would hate to think how much you would see if you were back in the realm."

Stella smiled modestly. "I do wish I was there. That I could do more to help, instead of being stuck over here. But I must be here for a reason. So, I will make the most of it."

"I'll pass your message on to Broomhilda," Flix promised.

"And I'll try to get some sleep, so I'm ready for tomorrow." She smiled as she got back into bed.

This time her dreams were sharper. Brigid and Maisie were in the tavern in animated discussion with a group of people. She pulled her cloak around herself tightly before tapping Brigid on the shoulder. Her friend swung around, and although Brigid couldn't see her, she sensed her. From the first day they had met, the three ladies could read each other's minds, and Stella was hoping that Brigid could read hers even if she couldn't see her. Brigid gave a slight nod and a smile. Stella focused on what she wanted to tell them. The vision she had seen. The colour of the sky and the colours of the robes. Taking Brigid's nod as recognition and understanding of the messages Stella was sharing, she changed her focus. Concentrating on where she was now. Flix, the hooded figure, the café, and the note with the cryptic message. Brigid nodded again.

Stella watched as Brigid turned to Maisie, in amongst the animated crowd and with a single glance communicated so much. Maisie turned to face exactly where Stella was standing and smiled, before turning back to the group. Satisfied that her friends understood, Stella brought herself back to the room. As she was floating back, something pulled her away. She found herself in the forest where she first met another coven in her dreams, at the beginning of her journey into the realm of magic.

Luna, Catherine and Tizzie looked up straight away, even though Stella's cloak was still in place. As the three women embraced her, she felt the familiar electrical charge when her magic surged. She was mindful that she was not supposed to be using her magic. She smiled at her friends and slowed her breathing.

"What happened?" Catherine asked. "We heard you disappeared, that you were taken away. No one could find you. Are you safe? Do you know about what is happening here? We were supposed to meet Brigid and Maisie tonight for the celebration of the new moon, but chaos broke out. Lots of people moving around on the roads. We decided to stay here and communicate through the flames."

"There were two travellers, who took me away from your realm into my world. To a place where I know no one. I'm okay. Although I'm not supposed to use my magic. There's someone watching me. Her name is Kai. Broomhilda also has one of the sprites looking out for me." Stella paused. The others nodded for her to continue. "There is a group in your world, gathering under a red and purple sky. I don't know what they are up to, but it's not a good feeling. I've found a place here that may be connected. I'm going to investigate tomorrow. I may be able to report back more tomorrow night. I really should go back now, although I would rather stay."

"Yes, it is wise to stop using your magic for now. Stay safe friend," Catherine said as they let go and Stella slowly, softly drifted back to her bed.

Being cautious is not the same as living in fear. Biding my time is a useful skill. Patience is a useful skill. An awareness of what is going on around me, that is key to my own self-awareness. Not being self-absorbed, but paying attention to the messages, the symbols and signs in the everyday. Waiting for opportunities, creating opportunities to learn and grow. The beginning of spell casting, the beginning of magic.

The Laundrette

Stella

"You are amazing Baz!" Stella hugged the barista as he handed her a coffee. "I loved the package on the doorstep too."

"I thought you might like it." He shrugged. "Especially after your stroll around the area."

"I have to go out for a while at lunch time today," Stella reminded him.

He nodded. "Mae's coming in you while you're out. We have it covered."

"I can work back later today if you need me to. I noticed we're open later the next few days," Stella offered, feeling guilty for leaving in the middle of their busy lunch rush.

"It does get busy in the afternoon, later in the week. I am not sure why; it's just how it's always been. Monday and Tuesday are our quiet days. The rest of the week is often crazy busy, from first thing until we close," Baz confirmed.

"Busy is good," Stella agreed.

Feeling like her feet were made of lead, for Stella the time seemed to be standing still. She checked the clock above the coffee machine a few times, to make sure it was working properly. It wasn't due to a lack of customers, but rather that Stella wanted the morning over, so she could see what was happening at 33 Main Street. Finally, it was one o'clock. She had timed the walk yesterday and knew it would take a maximum of ten minutes to walk to the laundrette. She waited until quarter past the hour before taking off her apron. With a quick wave to Baz and Mae, she ducked out between the customers.

With her heart in her chest, she felt guilty for leaving the café at such a busy time. Reaching Main Street, she remembered that she had forgotten to ask Baz for the location of a second-hand clothing shop. She scanned the street; there was a second chance shop, next door to the laundrette. How did she miss that yesterday? Stella wandered in and picked out a couple of shirts. A green one and a purple one that looked like they would fit her.

It was twenty-five minutes past one when she pushed open the door of the laundrette. Stella was surprised to find the space was taken up with washing machines and dryers. There was nothing mysterious or sinister looking. A few chairs were scattered around the walls of the area, for people to sit on while they waited for their washing. She placed her clothes into the closest machine. Fishing three two-dollar coins from her pocket she slid them into the coin slot. As she pressed the button to start the washing cycle, she scanned the shop. There were two other people in the building. They both appeared to be simply waiting for their machines to finish. One male; one female. Both at least sixty years old, wearing old worn clothes. The woman was reading a magazine. There was a pile of old worn and tattered magazines about fashion, or fancy homes on a nearby table. A walking stick was propped up next to her chair. The man was slouched, half asleep, with a distinct smell of old booze and tobacco. Both customers looked like they need-ed a shower and a good feed. Stella's stomach lurched at the smell of urine mixed with cheap wine. She looked around for a window to open, hoping to let in some fresh air. There were none that opened, the only windows being the narrow floor to ceiling glass panel next to the front door. She sat down so she could watch for anyone entering the build-ing.

From her position she could see a smaller second door, hidden on the opposite wall. Stella's heart pounded as she sat waiting for something to happen, feeling a little claustrophobic. She checked the time on her phone. It was exactly one thirty. The back door opened. Two women dressed in long black dresses and tall high heeled black boots walked through the door. Their dark and blonde hair respectively pulled back into tight buns—the type of hairdo Stella had created in her ballerina daughter's hair, every Friday of school term for years. They walked in silence to the third washing machine in the second row. The machine with the 'out of order' sign on the lid. Blondie lifted the lid. She took a small package out of a pocket in her dress and placed it in the washing machine. Dark Hair unwrapped a black shawl from her shoulders. She dropped the shawl on top of the package and closed the lid.

The women walked back through the door without speaking or acknowledging anyone. The door shut firmly behind them. The customers who were waiting for their rinse cycles to finish didn't appear to pay any attention to what had just occurred. With butterflies threatening to burst out of her stomach, Stella walked over to the machine. The lid creaked. She cringed, not wanting to draw any attention to herself. Neither of the oldies moved or indicated they cared what she was doing. Leaving the shawl in the machine, she picked up the parcel and slid it into the pocket of her coat. She glanced nervously at the back door, debating whether to wait for her clothes to finish their cycle before leaving the laundrette.

What seemed like an eternity was less than five minutes according to the clock on the wall. Stella mustered all her willpower to quieten the threat of sparks of magic which may uncontrollably overflow from her hands. The thud, thud, thud of the clothes spinning in the machine provided a distraction. Stella forced herself sit quietly with her hands crossed. She decided against drying her clothes. She didn't want to stay any longer than was absolutely necessary. Someone would probably be in soon to grab the package from the 'out of order' machine. The old man's and the elderly woman's machines finished within seconds of each other. Without acknowledging each other, they shuffled to their machines. Pain creasing the man's face as he reached in to get out his washing. Feeling helpless she wished she could help them. She watched as they collected their washing, shoving the clothes into their plastic bags. The door banged twice, as they left by the front door. Stella jumped each time. What where their stories? She stared at the machine with her clothes in it. She willed it to finish. She had chosen the quick cycle, which seemed to be taking forever. She hadn't needed to wash those two items, but it seemed a good idea at the time. A reason for entering the laundrette. A deep breath, to calm her nerves. Less than five minutes left. Intuition told her not to grab her clothes and run. She flicked through a magazine to distract herself.

A tall lady in a long, black trench coat strode through the front door. She opened the machine that had contained the parcel. Stella's heart skipped a beat. The lady peered inside, feeling around the barrel. She shook the shawl in case there was anything tangled in it. Stella buried her head in the magazine about country furnishings. Reading about the marvels of chalk paint. Several loud noises told Stella the lady was opening and slamming shut the lid of each of the other machines. The exception being the one shaking and swirling Stella's clothes. Muttering to herself, glancing furiously around the laundrette, the lady turned and stormed out the way she came.

Forcing herself to breath slowly, Stella stood up and stretched. She glanced casually out through the front window. The lady in the trench coat was talking to an older woman, also dressed in black, her grey hair tied back in a severe bun. Both women were waving their arms around, pointing at the laundrette. Stella sat back down. From her spot she could still see the women. A few seconds later, the older woman stormed off and the first lady walked towards the laundrette.

Stella's machine finally stopped. She jumped as the washing machine signalled her clothes were ready. Busying herself with her clothes, she ignored the sound of the door slamming open. As she folded her shirts, she heard the back door slam. Without waiting for anyone else to return, she quickly left the building.

Hurrying but not running, Stella made her way to the café. She dumped her coat and bag of clothes in the corner. She quickly donned her apron as she busied herself clearing the tables. As she smiled at Baz and Mae, her heart slowed to a more normal rate. The energy coursing through her body pulsating at a reduced rate. No threat of danger here in the café. Could she be sure of that? She wasn't sure if Flix had followed and witnessed the events of the afternoon. Or Kai.

The clock told her it was only just two o'clock in the afternoon. The whole event had taken less than thirty minutes. A steady stream of customers, smiling, joking, and jostling for their mid-afternoon caffeine fix kept her busy. It was dark by the time she opened the door to her flat.

The butterflies flitting in her stomach were competing with the coffee and chocolate bar she had consumed at the end of her shift. She gently pulled the parcel out of her coat. What had possessed her to steal the parcel out of the washing machine and bring it home? If this was a magical item, might it have some kind of tracking device? She was lucky the scary lady hadn't searched her. Or stalked her and stolen the package from her coat.

Stella untied the string, unfolding the brown paper parcel, carefully, like birthdays when she was little and would keep the paper to use in craft. Inside the fine layers of pink tissue paper lay three crystal wands. Stella gasped at their simplicity, their beauty. Subtle green and purple hues, vibrating with energy. Fluorite was used to transmute negative energy into positive energy. In healing it was used to absorb negative energy. Aiding people with burnout. Why three wands? Each wand easily fitted in the palm of her hand.

"I do feel guilty that I took these," she told Flix as he came over. "The women who were looking for them were scary. Extremely annoyed that they couldn't find their parcel. What I don't understand, is why all the secrecy for a few wands? I'm sure these are available to buy anywhere."

"These don't look like regular fluorite wands," Flix said as he inspected the crystals. "See the gold flecks the silver thread? There is something odd about these wands. Do you have your phone? Can you take a photo for Broomhilda?"

"Of course." Stella took several shots of the wands, from different angles. "Broomhilda doesn't have a mobile phone, does she?"

"She doesn't. I was thinking you should probably try and reach her during your dreams tonight. Whoever kidnapped you, will likely know by now that you have been using your magic. The hooded figure is sure to have seen some of the energy surges and reported them. I can watch over you while you sleep to make sure you are okay. If that sounds reasonable to you." Flix looked at the crystals from his position at the edge of the table. "These look important. I think she will want to know about these wands."

"Well then, let's get started. I'll aim for Brigid's tavern. I know my friends will pass the message on to Broomhilda." Holding the crystals gingerly she asked, "Should I take these too?"

Eyeing the fluorite, Flix replied, "Better not. We don't know what they are exactly. I don't know what would happen if you took them through the portal in your dreams. I can let Broomhilda know to get to Brigid's tavern as soon as possible. While you put those somewhere safe."

Quickly wrapping up the wands, Stella tucked the parcel in the vegetable crisper in the fridge. "It felt like the right place for them, the safest place, just in case," she responded to Flix's questioning gaze.

"It is as good a place as any," Flix agreed. "Broomhilda should be there at the tavern when you get there, if my message made it through to her."

With her coat on and her phone in the pocket, Stella lay down on the bed and closed her eyes. She remembered that first day, the beginning of her adventure. She had closed her eyes and followed her intuition, finding a portal in the bottom of her garden. She slowed her breathing. *Believe in myself. Believe I can do this. Picture the tavern.* This time Stella had a reference point.

"Stella!" Hearing her friends' voices and feeling their embrace, her energy increased intensity, vibrating inside every cell of her body. Stella opened her eyes.

"I'm so pleased to see you both. It feels like forever since we shared a tankard and a chat. Unfortunately, I can't stay long. Someone's spying on me. Flix is keeping me safe while I'm here," she added seeing the concern on her friends faces. "Is Broomhilda here too?"

"Yes!" Broomhilda waved from the top of the bar.

"I followed the clue I was given. To a laundrette. A shop where people wash their clothes if they can't wash them at home. I don't yet know the significance of that location." Stella passed her phone to Broomhilda. "Here is a photo of some wands I found there. Two women, dressed in long robes, entered the shop, and hid these, wrapped in a scarf, in one of the machines for washing clothes. I don't know why I did it, but as soon as they left, I picked the parcel up out of the machine and hid it in my coat," Stella spoke quickly, words tumbling over each other in her haste to tell her story. "Another woman came in looking for the parcel, and when it wasn't there, she was angry. She spoke to another woman, they both looked annoyed. Not necessarily evil, but I wouldn't want to get into an argument with them. I don't think any of them realised that I am the one who took these. I am sure if they did, they would have followed me home and I wouldn't be here telling you my story."

Her friends scrutinised the photos she had taken. "Where are the wands now?" Broomhilda asked.

"In my fridge, in the flat where I am staying," she responded. "I didn't know what else to do with them. Flix said there was something odd about them. As you can see, they are fluorite, with gold and silver entwined through each one. He said they possessed stronger magic than merely transforming negative energy into positive energy. Because of the gold and silver woven into them."

"Flix is correct. He knows a significant amount about crystals and their attributes." Broomhilda studied the photo. Passing the phone back to Stella, she continued, "It is very old magic that can add metal to crystals. Doing so can modify the properties of the stone. In this instance it will enhance its strength, changing negative energy into positive, and possibly transforming positive energy into negative." She frowned as she considered the possibility.

"What can we do?" asked Brigid.

"You and Maisie can warn as many people as you can to be wary of strangers. To be cautious around anyone who is behaving strangely. Not to enter into conversation. Make sure we don't move too far from home. This is the opposite of how we normally interact in this realm, but for now it is the best option. We stay close to each other. There is safety in numbers." She turned to Stella.

"You need to return the wands to the place where you took them. Continue to work at the cafe, for now. Flix will stay with you. We will send additional help immediately should you need it. I will send someone to see who picks up the wands."

"What if whoever owns the wands are waiting at the laundrette, to see if anyone tries to return the wands?" Maisie worried, fidgeting with her necklace. Made from amethyst, rose quartz and tigers' eye, it was one of the many necklaces she designed. Those she made for Brigid and Stella had an extra layer of connection and protection.

"It's okay Maisie, I will be careful." Stella hoped she sounded more confident than she felt. Her friends were adept at reading her mind as well as her body language. "The sign on the door said the laundrette is open twenty-four hours a day. If I return the wands now, while it is dark, it will be easier to sneak in and out without being seen." Stella turned to Broomhilda. "Is it possible for Flix to meet me in Main Street, with the wands? I travelled here in my dreams, not through a portal. Is there a way to get me to the laundrette?" Stella faltered, not sure if she was making sense.

Broomhilda answered, "There is a way. Flix will be waiting for you, near the laundrette. Do you remember that first time, when you created a portal yourself and arrived in the middle of the tavern?" Stella nodded, thinking back to that day. She succeeded the first time, literally landing in the middle of a tavern full of people.

"You can perform that same spell now. Picture the laundrette, in as much detail as you can remember from your visit. Focus on the place you want to meet Flix," Broomhilda instructed. "Feel yourself stopping into the flat and picking up your body as you go. You can do this by tapping into the energy of your body." The fairy turned to Brigid, "Does the portal out the back still work?" she asked her.

Brigid nodded. "It worked a few days ago, when we went looking for Stella."

"Excellent!" Broomhilda said. "There's no time for goodbyes, you will be back here with your friends soon. Now go out that door and return those wands. Flix will keep us updated." For a fairy, Broomhilda could be forceful; no one ever argued.

Stella smiled at her friends. As she turned to the door, she focused on the atmosphere of her flat and the laundrette. Only recently she had discovered her ability to tune in to a place. Reading its atmosphere as she read people's auras and emotions. A feeling, a smell, a sense of the space, the age of a building. Not something she could easily describe to others.

WITH A JOLT, STELLA connected with her body at the same time as she landed in a dark laneway. Like a sudden stop on a carnival fun ride, the action temporarily winded her. Traffic noises from the main street sounded close. As dizziness threatened to overcome her, she connected with the ground through her palms. The rough paved surface cool beneath her skin. Her body vibrated, as if connected to the ground deep below the surface.

"That's new," she muttered to herself.

"Are you okay?" Even though she was expecting the sprite to join her, her body jumped at the sound of the tiny voice beside her.

"I think so," Stella answered, relieved that Flix was by her side. He may not be a warrior but as moral support he was just perfect.

"You landed with quite a thud," he replied. "It was easy to find you."

"I hope no one else noticed." Stella glanced around half expecting to see someone lurking in the shadows behind the row of shops. Thank you for meeting me here with these." she took the package Flix was holding and tucked it in the pocket of her coat.

"Let's be quick and get out of here," Flix said nervously. "There is no back door, so we will have to go through the front. There are a couple of customers in there, I think they are taking a nap, rather than washing their clothes."

"That's strange," Stella murmured, "Inside the laundrette there is definitely another door. I thought it led outside. Two people came through it and left by it too. Maybe there is a back room?"

"We can work that out later, for now, let's get in and get out." Flix's firm tone left no doubt in her mind. Broomhilda had taught the sprite well. Before her twitching nerves overwhelmed her, Stella straightened herself to full height. held her head high and walked through the door. Flix waited outside, in the shadows, keeping an eye on what was happening inside.

The only two people in the laundrette, were both curled up as best they could on separate chairs. One dryer was spinning, with the rhythmic click as the drum circled with clothes inside. The washing machine was just as noisy. Neither of the customers paid the slightest bit of attention to Stella.

Relieved the machine in the middle of the row was free, the out of order sign still propped on the lid. Stella exhaled excitedly. She had been worried that it would be in use when she was hoping to hide the wands. *Slow breathing. Walk to the machine. No one is awake. Open the lid quietly. Place the parcel in. Leave quietly.* She spoke herself through the whole activity. A quick glance to the far wall confirmed a door.

There was no light outside in the alley. The glow of light snaking out from under the door indicated a back room. Stella was curious as to what was on the other side. Remembering Flix's words to be quick, she reluctantly left the mystery of the door for another day and exited the building.

"How did it go?" Flix whispered as he appeared in the pocket of her coat.

"Easy. Although I was tempted to go through that door and see what was on the other side," Stella replied. "Do we stay to see who picks up the parcel?"

"No! I have strict instructions to make sure you get home safely to the flat."

She knew she wasn't going to win that argument, for now. "I am tired." She yawned.

"You need some sleep. I get the feeling tomorrow is going to be a busy day." Stella silently agreed with Flix's words.

Magic is about what we can see and manifest, but also about what we cannot see. A chance encounter. A surprise in the mail. A telephone call. Finding something that was lost. We open ourselves up to the possibilities that there is more to life than merely existing. We do have a purpose. We do matter. We can make a difference. We look beyond the normal, to the magic just beyond. We look through the portal. We are captivated by what we see. We awaken the dream, hidden deep inside us. We begin our journey of discovery.

The Fire

S tella

Stella was startled out of a dream, not knowing where she was. And what was that awful noise?

Alarm bells were literally sounding in her ears. In the haze of sleep, Stella wasn't sure where she was or what the noise was. She reached for her clock to turn off the rather loud alarm. The beeping continued. It took a few seconds to realise it was the fire alarm downstairs.

She leapt out of bed, noticing she was still wearing her shirt and jeans from the day before. As Stella slipped her shoes on, Flix said from his position on the windowsill, "I'll keep an eye out from up here. Go, but be careful, and don't do anything stupid." Grabbing her coat, because it had her phone, and because it was magic, never know when it might come in handy. Stella bounded down the stairs, grabbing the railing to steady herself as she tripped four stairs from the bottom.

Baz was already in the kitchen, flapping a tea towel at the flames leaping out of the stove, lapping up the walls. Smoke was swirling around, trying to find an escape. The heat of the flames, the smell of the smoke, the air thick with smoke stinging her eyes, was making it difficult to get her bearings. Baz put his hand on her arm. Stella could feel his anxiety, oozing from every pore of his body. "I was going to pour water on the fire, but something stopped me."

"Baz I'm so glad you didn't. You don't pour water on an electrical fire!" Stella observed the flames, which were getting angrier as they snaked up the wall to the ceiling. "We need to leave. Let the fire brigade put out this fire." She heard the sirens in the distance and hoped they were coming to help them.

"I must let Mae know. She's staying with her mother in Ipswich I think, for a couple of days. Her mother had a fall." Baz sounded panicked. Stella held his arm and steered him through the door into the café, leading him out of the front door of the café. Baz kept trying to drag her back inside. "I have to save the café, for Mae and her family," he protested loudly.

"We can let her know once we're a safe distance away. She wouldn't want you to get hurt, trying to save the café." She spoke gently, trying her best to calm him.

"I guess so," Baz agreed. He stopped suddenly, like a child who needed dragging to safety. At least he had stopped trying to return to the kitchen. Three firemen hurried past them and into the café. Stella gently helped Baz to an area just outside the closest convenience store, near the parked fire engine.

"Excuse me, were you inside?" A paramedic touched Stella on the arm. Stella estimated that she was in her mid-twenties, with long brown hair tied up in a high ponytail. Her name, according to her shirt, was Emma.

"Yes, we were. Baz was trying to put out the fire, but it was too much. The smoke was too thick. It was difficult to see what we were doing. Breathing was a little challenging too. We decided the best thing was to leave it to the firemen to deal with," Stella replied.

"You're both very lucky," Emma confirmed as they sat on the seat near the ambulance. "Neither of you show any signs of being injured, burnt, or suffering from smoke inhalation. We could monitor you at the hospital if you prefer." A noise escaped Baz's lips. A squeaky gasp for air. Emma patted Baz on the arm. "Do you suffer from anxiety?" she asked softly.

Baz nodded, his hands twisting the tea towel he was still holding. He looked like he was going to burst into tears, Stella reached out and held his hand.

He shook his head, lightly rocking back and forth. "I don't understand how it happened. I walked into the kitchen to start setting up for the day. The fat in a saucepan on the stove had caught fire. I don't understand how. I know I turned everything off last night. I always double check that, always," muttered Baz.

"Let the firemen sort that out. I think you should probably come to the hospital for a few hours' observation." Seeing the horrified look on Baz's face, she continued. "Or if you feel okay, you could go home and rest. Do you have anyone at home who can look after you for the next twenty-four hours?"

"I can't go to the hospital, and I can't go home!" Baz exclaimed. "I need to tidy up the café, and make sure the kitchen and the café are ready when we open for business." Baz looking around wildly, horrified at the thought.

"What if we both stayed?" Stella asked. "I can look after Baz. We can get breakfast from a café down the road. I'll make sure he doesn't work too hard. That he stays calm."

Emma looked from Baz to Stella. Stella appeared as calm as Baz was flustered. "I guess that's fine," she said grudgingly. "Promise me you'll stay with him all day and that you'll take him to the hospital if his anxiety gets any worse."

"I promise," Stella said solemnly. "We won't go back into the café until the firemen declare it as safe to do so."

"YOU WERE LUCKY." THE biggest of the three firemen walked over to the group. Emma waved as she hopped into the ambulance and drove off. The other two fireman were at the back of their fire truck, rolling up the giant hoses. On the horizon behind them Stella noticed a strange crimson tinge to the sunrise. She was distracted by the fireman and didn't pay the strange colour any attention. "The police will be here soon to take your statements," the fireman continued.

"Police! Why?" Baz stood up again. She had only just managed to calm him down. She shot the fireman an angry look.

"I am sure it is just routine," Stella soothed Baz. She turned to the fireman. "Do you know what caused the fire and how much damage there is?" she asked, hoping she sounded more efficient than she felt.

"That's the strange thing." The fireman took off his helmet and scratched his head. He placed it back on his head, crookedly. He looked like a kindly old uncle. Stella supressed a grin. Reading his name tag, she prompted. "What was strange, Dave?"

"The stove wasn't turned on, but the fat in the saucepan on the stove was the source of the fire. It makes no sense. It's like there was a surge of energy that heated up the fat causing it to catch fire. It's likely to have been an electrical fault. We have someone investigating it," Dave replied.

"Do you think it was an accident?" Nausea rose in her throat. Was it her fault? Had her energy as she travelled through the realms somehow caused the fire? She slowed her breathing, calming her energy. Next to her, Baz started shaking. She realised he was crying. "It will be okay," she whispered, hugging him.

Dave pointed to a man coming out of the café and waved him over. "This is Steve, he'll double check everything and write his report. Who should he talk to? Are you the owner?" he asked Stella.

"The owner is away, looking after her mother," Stella responded. "You can talk to me, and I'll pass on the information to her." She turned her attention to Steve. "This might be a silly question, but do you know when the café will be okay to open again?" Baz stopped sobbing and looked over at Steve hopefully.

"You'll need to get an electrician in to test the electricity and confirm it's safe. You'll also need a new stove unit. A builder to make any repairs. A new coat of paint for the kitchen. All of that, you would be lucky to be open again in a couple of weeks. Coordinating tradesmen is a nightmare." Steve grinned. "I'll have my report done in an hour. You won't be able to make a start inside until the police have finished their investigation." He walked over to Dave. "I want you to come and have a look at something."

Baz straightened up. "Two weeks? That's such a long time. Do you think we can get all this fixed in a week? What if we can't find tradesmen to help us? What will Mae say?" Stella could tell Baz was in danger of tears again.

"We can do anything we set our mind to," Stella told him. "We'll start by working on the things that are in our control." She stood up. "While we wait for the police, we can ring Mae. We need to let her know what is going on. If you and Mae are happy with it, I can coordinate everything. I have had experience with this sort of thing. Managing projects," she said, seeing Baz was about to ask her something.

I saw the relief wash over his face. "Thank goodness you're here. I can help but I'm not an in-charge sort of person. I'm a worker, and a people person."

"They are both great assets Baz. Don't sell yourself short. Why don't you go and grab us coffees and toasties from the *Awesome Bean's Café*? After we eat, you can talk to any customers that come by and tell them what's going on. Here's some money for brekky. Can I have your phone to ring Mae? you have her number in your phone, right?"

Baz gave Stella a hug. "You're a lifesaver." He handed over his phone, and took the money Stella held out. She watched him walk the short distance to the café, making sure he made it inside safely. Baz was probably ten years older than she was. She felt protective of him. He was vulnerable. Another ability she seemed to have acquired, was a heightened sense of others' emotions.

Stella was concerned she was the cause of the fire. Fireman Dave thought a surge of energy was the cause of the fire, in a stove that had been turned off. She suspected that travelling through time and space may have caused the stove to malfunction. But now wasn't the time to dwell on it. She pressed the green button next to Mae's number on Baz's phone.

MAE SOUNDED STRESSED, but also relieved that Stella offered to take charge. "Mum's not doing so well after her fall. I must stay with her until I can find alternative arrangements for her care. The doctors have recommended that she needs ongoing full-time care. It looks like a retirement home is the best option for her. Not that she agrees now. I need to find one that she will agree to, which won't be easy." Stella listened sympathetically to Mae's dilemma.

"If you're comfortable with me taking charge of things here, I'm happy to. I have experience managing people and projects. I'll look after Baz too. He's really stressed at the moment. He feels responsible for the fire, even though he did nothing wrong," Stella told Mae.

"Yes, Baz is such a softie. He wants to help everyone. He also tends to worry a lot. I'm more than happy for you to take the lead on this Stella, if you're comfortable to do so." Mae paused, and added excitedly, "One of the benefits of living locally my entire life and being part of a big family means that I have a few relatives who are tradesmen. I can get the people you need far more quickly than you would think. Leave it with me."

Stella thought that was promising, as long as the fire and police report were positive.

"Mae said she was going to contact her cousins who are tradies. She was sure they would be able to help us," Stella told Baz when he returned with the coffees, sandwiches, and a bag full of treats.

"Carmen and Deo said they would help us after work, when they close up for the day, if we need them to." Baz looked a lot happier, now that he had spoken to his friends. "As well as our brekky, they packed us a bag of treats to nibble on during the day. Free of charge." He handed Stella's money back to her. "They insisted."

"That was nice of them," Stella said, taking a long sip of the coffee. "Great coffee. Not as great as yours, but good enough."

That made Baz smile. "We've known each other for years. Carmen, Deo, and I were at barista training together. Deo and I worked in pubs for a while too. These days it's easier to get up early. Working until early in the morning and dealing with rowdy drunk customers isn't fun anymore. Our customers today can be rowdy, but only until they get their coffee."

Stella unwrapped her toastie. From their position, seated on the bench closest to the café, they could watch the door. When customers came to see what was going on, or in the hope of their morning caffeine fix, Baz would get up and talk to them. Interacting with his regulars was keeping him calm and focused. Stella knew the type well. Needed to feel needed. She wondered how long he had been working with Mae. He thrived on that contact and connection with others. Under different circumstances, she would ask him what his life story was.

Steve was the only fireman left at the scene. He had arrived after the first responders, in his own vehicle. He was talking to a police officer. As they existed the café, they were comparing notes, referring to the notes scribbled on pages of their notebooks. Stella wanted to walk over to them and find out what they were saying. Instead, she reassuringly patted Baz on his arm. They ate their breakfast in silence.

"Stella? Steve said I should come and talk to you." The police officer walked over. "My name is Kellie."

Stella stood and held out her hand. "Yes, I'm Stella. The owner Mae, is out of town, looking after an unwell family member. She's asked me to be her spokesperson. I'll relay all information to her, and she'll make any decisions that need to be made. I'm coordinating this for her with all the emergency services and any tradies we may need."

"Steve tested the stove. Even though you turned it off yesterday, it did cause the fire. It pays to check all electrical appliances regularly. Frayed wiring within elements in the stove caused the electrical fault, which led to the fire. It was likely caused by wear and tear over time." Kellie handed Stella a copy of the report. "You were lucky. There is a lot of smoke damage, and the fire has left its mark. Overall though, not a lot of repairs required. It could have been much worse. It appears this was no one's fault. You will need to confirm all the electrics are checked and fixed, and the stove is replaced. Then, after any structural damage is rectified, and you make any cosmetic updates, you can re-open the café. Ensure that all the work is signed by the relevant professional and keep all the paperwork."

Baz's smile would have given the cheshire cat a run for its money. He clapped his hands in happiness, before giving Stella a huge hug. She was thankful that Baz chose to hug her instead of the policewoman. It was going to be a busy day.

AS IT WAS ALREADY ELEVEN in the morning when Kellie gave Stella and Baz the news that they could begin the clean-up. "Why don't we go and grab some lunch before we start in the café?" suggested Stella.

Baz perked up at the idea of seeing Carmen and Deo again. "Terrific idea."

Mae sent a text that her cousins, an electrician, and a builder, would be calling in sometime in the afternoon. Her text apologised that she couldn't get her painter cousin until early next week. Stella reassured Mae that her and Baz would be able to paint the parts of the kitchen that needed it.

An hour later, during which Baz's friends had both calmed and energised Baz, they returned to the café.

Every surface was coated in a fine layer of wet soot. Baz stacked the tables and chairs in one corner of the café. He wiped each piece of furniture as he did so. His cloth and bucket of water were already a dirty grey colour after half a dozen chairs. Stella eyed the water in her mop bucket. It was the same murky colour. It was going to take several passes at mopping and wiping down furniture before it was clean. All the food would have to be thrown out. Stella kept that horrible thought to herself for now. One bite of the elephant at a time. She cringed, as another unpleasant thought slapped her in the face. It was horrid that her energy may have been the cause of the fire. What if someone else had started that fire, in the hope of injuring her, or keeping her out of the way? How could she work out if this were true or a figment of her overactive imagination?

She plopped the mop back in the bucket and straightened up. Something moved and caught her eye. She recognised the little figure, frantically waving from outside the kitchen window. "Flix!" she gasped before she could stop herself.

"What was that?" Baz asked from the other side of the room, wiping down one of the larger tables.

"Now that we're starting to get this under control, I'm just going to pop upstairs and see if there's any damage in the flat. I told Mae I'd let her know if we need to repair anything there," she replied.

"I'll come up too," Baz offered, dropping his cloth into the bucket. Stella knew he felt vulnerable and scared after the fire, but that he also wanted to protect her. She smiled at him.

"Thanks, but I'll be okay. Can you stay here in case anyone comes in? We need to make sure all the customers stay out until we're open again. Of course, if the police, the fireys, or the tradesmen arrive, please let them in. I won't be long." Baz would freak if he saw Flix and he'd experienced enough surprises for one day. She wasn't sure what might be waiting for her at the top of the stairs. Stella was halfway up the steps when she heard the familiar voice.

"Where do you think you are going?" Stella looked down to see Flix sitting on the step in front of her. He smiled. "I have been keeping an eye on you and Baz. There's no damage from smoke or fire in the flat. I was able to stop the fire getting into your room. Ancient magic—a charm spell we are taught in school can protect a space from the elements."

"Thank goodness! Thank you." Stella wondered if she could hug the sprite, or if she would crush him.

"No hugging!" Flix rolled his eyes. "Of course I can read your mind."

"Does Broomhilda know what happened?" Stella asked, sitting down next to Flix.

"Yes. At least she knows that there was a fire. It wasn't your energy that caused the fire. You were asleep when it started. Broomhilda is working on the theory that someone followed you from the laundrette. They didn't want to hurt you, but rather they were likely trying to distract you from figuring out their plan."

"If that's what they intended, then it worked beautifully. It's going to take us days to get the café cleaned up. Baz is a mess. I won't be ducking out at lunchtime to check out that door in the laundrette." Stella sighed and stood up. "I had better get back to Baz. I don't want to leave him alone for too long. I'll try to get to the laundrette later this afternoon. After Baz heads home for the day."

Flix stared up at Stella tiny hands on his hips. She supressed the urge to giggle. He may have thought he was giving her a cranky stare, but it didn't quite work. "I'll check in with you for any news from the other realm, before I go wandering," she promised.

STELLA STUMBLED AS she walked through from the kitchen to the restaurant. Exhausted by her escapades the previous evening. She glanced down at her feet, unexpectedly finding a long thin piece of metal was sticking through the floorboards. She bent to pick it up before it caused an injury to anyone else. It looked like an old ornate hat pin. She thought it was odd, and popped it on the bench, to ask Baz about it later. She heard him speaking to Mae on his mobile. "We have the fire department's report. The fire was an accident. There was an issue with the stove, although they aren't exactly sure why or what triggered the problem. The police report says pretty much the same thing, that no one was at fault. Stella and I are cleaning up." Baz paused, listening to Mae.

Baz passed the phone to Stella. "Baz has been amazing. He's cleaned absolutely everything in the kitchen and the restaurant area, and he's spoken to all the customers who have called in to ask what was happening and if we were okay. Everyone has been so positive and helpful."

Handing the mobile back to Baz, she told him, "Mae wanted me to pass on a huge thanks to you Baz. She's so relieved we are both okay, and that the café can reopen once we get the wiring fixed up. She was a little stressed that her cousins couldn't get here today. They promised her tomorrow, definitely. She's disappointed that she wasn't there helping them. I say we deserve a break and refreshments. I'm going out for a coffee. Do you want one?"

"One too many coffees for me today already," Baz replied. "I'd love an orange juice if they have one."

Stella noted how busy the street was. Unusually so. A few people appeared to be staring at the café. It wasn't every day we have a fire in the street. A figure across the street caught Stella's eye. Her memory wasn't firing on all cylinders. The woman was dressed in a long black dress, stockings, and sneakers. Had she seen her at the laundrette? Was she a customer? Or just someone she'd passed in the street? Stella hurried the few metres to the *Awesome Beans* café. Her heart pounded, worried at leaving Baz alone. The mystery of what lurked behind the rear door haunted her. *Later.*

"No charge for you Stella. You and Baz are doing a great job, getting the café sorted out. Just between you and me, I don't know how Baz would have handled today, if you weren't around. He is a terrific person, but not a leader, or an organiser." Deo tucked his hand behind his back leaving Stella nowhere to hand over money for her purchases. "Your shout when we call in to check out *The Friendly Cup* next week."

Stella smiled her thanks and left Deo and Carmen to deal with the additional customers triggered by the unexpected closure of Mae's café. They shared many of the same local clientele. "It's good to see there is no fierce competition between our cafes," Stella commented as she handed Baz a bottle of orange juice.

"There can be," Baz replied. "But around here we all band together when anyone is in trouble. Ever since the floods back twelve years ago. We share a healthy rivalry, working together when we need to."

THE UPDATE FROM MAE was short and to the point. *Good news. The electrician will be there first thing in the morning. With the new stove. He will check the wiring and the circuitry. We should have power back on by midday. Builder tomorrow too, he promises.*

The sudden drop in temperature indicated that it would soon be dark inside the café. The ambience created by the lack of windows felt eerie without lighting.

Stella gently prised the cleaning cloth from Baz's grip. "We can finish the cleaning tomorrow morning, and get the painting done after the tradesmen complete their work."

Reluctantly letting Stella drop the cloth into the bucket of eucalypt disinfectant water, Baz pointed to her flat, "Are you going to be okay up there all by yourself?"

"Of course! You don't need to worry about me. I'm going to go for a walk. Maybe grab some dinner. What about you? Do you have anyone at home?" Stella asked, closing the front doors, making sure all the power sockets were switched off. Just in case.

"Two cats, five fish and a canary. Lots of little mouths to feed, and I have so much to tell them about today. I'll be fine." Baz smiled. "I feel so much better now. You are a terrific friend Stella. Thank you for being here today and keeping everything on track." Baz hugged her. "I'll be here first thing in the morning."

"Me too. I'll walk with you to Main Street, that's the way you go home, isn't it?" Stella locked the back door, handing the key to Baz. "We work well together. Thank you for everything you did today. I couldn't have handled all this without you either."

"Observant lady, that is the way I walk to the bus. Can you look after the key for the café, just in case, as you live upstairs, and anything happens. You'll be here in the morning to let me in." Baz closed her hand over the key and took her arm. "Let's go!"

Stella watched as Baz climbed up the two stairs and found a seat on the already crowded bus. Her hand trembled a little. Stella steadied herself by placing her hands in the pocket of her coat. With a large gulp of air, she turned left. Marching purposefully towards the laundrette. *Oh no!* She was nearly at the second-hand shop when she remembered Flix. Her body felt like it was on fire. If she turned back now, she would likely lose her nerve. Her fingers crossed in her pockets, willing Flix to be close by.

Nearly tripping over the mess, the pile of clothes dumped outside the op shop gave her an idea. She held her breath, blocking out the aroma of unwashed clothes as she gathered some up in a bundle. She pushed open the door of the laundrette. Her heart skipped a beat; she didn't expect to find herself in the middle of a crowd.

She counted ten people with various degrees of boredom and impatience on their faces, baskets in hand, keen to have their washing done and head home after a busy day. Lucky customers found seats to await the completion of their machines to finish their whirring clunking cycles. A handful of those in the queue, were chatting as if it were a gathering of old friends. Focused on their task at hand no one paid any attention to Stella. Like a well-rehearsed play. Dirty clothes shoved into a machine. Lid shut and turned on. Wet clothes transferred to the dryer. Clean clothes folded into bags. All by rote, participants already planning dinner.

Stella gagged. Holding the clothes so tightly the smell was unbearable. She needed a distracted from the smell of old deodorant. There was little possibility of checking out what was behind the door unless she was able to follow someone else through it. Not bold enough to simply stride over and open the door. She was willing to wait for the right opportunity. She had her suspicions that it may be a portal to another realm, but she couldn't be sure.

"I know you." A lady standing near the door, caught her eye and spoke directly to Stella, "You work at that café that had the fire this morning." Everyone turned to look at her. So much for not drawing any attention to herself.

Stella made her way through the group to the woman who asked the question. A perfect excuse to get a closer look at the door. "Yes, I work with Baz and Mae. We should have the café open again in a few days." Her energy pulsed with anticipation. Close enough to the door, her magic felt the force of the magic contained behind it. Pushing her feet firmly on the floor to stop her toes curling. Trying to act as if the magic wasn't calling to hers.

"I'm Mabel." The woman smiled warmly. "My machine will be finished soon, but I think there is a line up for it." She shrugged eyeing the pile of clothes in Stella's arms. "So, I can't really offer it to you."

"I'm Stella. I'm in no hurry to get my washing done, apart from the smell that is. We found these clothes when we were cleaning up after the fire. I offered to wash them. Waiting for the machines to finish will give me a chance to rest after such a busy day. We're lucky there wasn't more damage, but there was black soot everywhere." Stella exaggerated. Was this woman simply waiting for her washing to dry? Or was she part of the sinister plot that had dragged Stella from the other realm?

"I need to get home and let my cat out for a walk before it gets dark," the woman said, shoving her dripping wet washing, straight from the machine into her shopping bag. "Air drying clothes is the best. I have a drying rack on my verandah. Nice to meet you, Stella." Mabel made her way through the group still waiting to wash their clothes, leaving via the front door.

Stella's stomach growled. A nervous rumble as much as hunger pains. It was still too crowded to try that door. Stella spied an empty seat near the back door. Plonking herself on it, she dumped the pile of clothes on the floor in front of her. She pulled her mobile out of her pocket to distract herself.

A couple of seconds later the front door swung open. "We have to close in five minutes," a loud voice boomed.

"I'm still waiting to use the machine!" grumbled a man to her left. She had noticed him when she walked in because his backpack was bright pink.

"My clothes are in the dryer," protested a young fit looking woman, dressed in designer sporting gear. Stella couldn't fathom why people spent lots of money on clothes to play sports in.

"Mine are in their rinse cycle," a young man dressed in a business suit complained. People started yelling at the tall man standing in the front doorway.

"We will give everyone here one hundred dollars, if you pick up your clothes and leave now." The woman spoke in a firm voice, a little softer than the man. Both dressed all in black - trousers, shirts, and boots. Stella turned to get a closer look. Neither of the figures looked familiar.

Those waiting in the laundrette scrambled to get their clothes out of the machines, eager to claim their money.

"There is no need to rush. There is enough money for everyone here," the woman continued. Stella waited until everyone else had claimed their money. She took her time picking the bundle of clothes up off the floor. Thankfully, she hadn't had to drag her clothes out of the machine, dripping wet, like the young man who had flown in on his skateboard and had left with a trail of water dripping behind him. Realising she could not procrastinate any longer, she made her way to the front door.

The woman stood in between Stella and the door. "Don't you want your money?" the woman asked.

"We had a fire in our café today. I was thinking about all the things I must do when I return; I'm a little distracted," Stella responded, as the lady handed her a pile of notes, almost pushing her out the door. Stella heard the door being locked as soon as her feet hit the footpath.

"Can you please put those clothes back where you found them? They stink!" Flix popped his head out of Stella's coat pocket.

"Flix! I'm so sorry that I forgot to see you after work. How did you get in there, and did you see what just happened?" Stella dumped the clothes back into one of the clothing bins outside the second-hand shop.

"I have my ways. Just don't forget me next time. You are lucky I keep an eye on you. I figured you would be distracted after today. I jumped into your pocket before you left with Baz." Flix smiled, softening his tone a little. "I did see and hear everything in the laundrette. I am sorry you didn't get to try that door. Maybe tomorrow. Let's get home, it has been a big day for you."

Casting a spell is partly setting intentions and finding the appropriate tools and ingredients, collecting symbols and items that represent the outcome we are aiming for. It is also about manipulating the elements of air, water, earth, and fire. It is about seasons, the cycles of the moon the phases and stages of our lives and our spirit.

It is magic as ancient as our land. As old as our world and those other worlds, and other realms that may live beside ours, or those that have lived before. It is that collective wisdom, passed down through the ages. New discoveries when we open our minds and our hearts. Discoveries of olden times kept alive by the new generation of people who believe. This is magic.

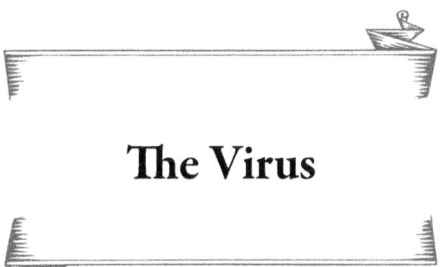

The Virus

S tella
  There was something niggling at the back of Stella's conscious-ness. Something important she needed to remember. Did the cupboard in the flat have similar magical properties to her coat? Perched on the shelf that was empty on the previous morning stood an old radio. "What are the chances that the batteries in this thing still work?" she said as Flix joined her at the table.

She needed to conserve battery power on her mobile. In case her girls needed to contact her. "I really should remember to pick up a phone charger," she told Flix as she flicked the power switch. It was early. Being able to wake up exactly when she needed to was a trick she had mastered back when she had kids to get ready for school.

"I don't know the number for the local radio station," Stella said, slowing turning the tuning knob until she heard the familiar crackle, and voices came into focus.

We are waking up to the incredible news that hundreds of people pre-sented to local hospitals in the last twelve hours. Symptoms of a severe al-lergic reaction, cause unknown. So far, the allergen seems to be contained to Australia. We will bring you the latest news as soon as more information becomes available.

"Oh, my goodness!" Stella exclaimed. "We're all only just recov-ering from the last pandemic." Her fingers trembled as she messaged her daughters. England seemed a long way away. Her girls didn't know about her other life or the other realm. As far as they knew she was still in her home, with her cat Puddles, her herb garden and working in the childcare centre.

The quick response from Andie was reassuring. *We are fine Mum, honestly. The weird pandemic thingy is only in Australia. Before you ask, Kay and Pedro are fine. They came to visit us just after Christmas and decided they liked it so much they are staying awhile. Hope you are okay, love from Emily and me.*

Her heart yearned to be in England. Grown up as they were, they were still her children. "I plan to visit them in the next few months. As long as this doesn't turn into another worldwide pandemic." Not hearing a reply from Flix, she looked at her friend.

"It appears what is happening here is also happening in our realm. Strange random illnesses, allergic reactions. I will have more details later once I talk to Broomhilda. Try not to worry," Flix said.

Stella smiled at Flix. "Thanks. I know it will be all right. I get the feeling that it is up to me to figure it out. I will somehow. For now, though I'm going downstairs. I want to open before Baz gets here. I promise I'll come back here, before I head to the laundrette."

Flix nodded. "I know you will."

Deciding to keep the radio on, in case there were updates, Stella sat it on the bench in the kitchen. Less than a minute later, the door swung open. The aroma of fresh coffee and toasties reminded Stella how hungry she was.

"Good morning!" Baz beamed. "I thought we could use a hearty breakfast before we start the day. Carmen and Deo gave us some of their famous caramel slice for dessert." Seeing the expression on her face, he added "Hey, are you okay?" Baz placed the cups and food on the table as he slid into the seat across from Stella.

"I'm fine. My kids are overseas. They are all grown up, but anyway, I was just checking in that they were okay. They are. Hang on, have you heard the news?" Stella picked up the coffee, "And thanks for the coffee and breakfast."

"You're welcome. Yes, the radio was on in the café when I got our brews. How did you hear the news? We have no electricity here."

"I found a battery powered radio in the cupboard. Surprisingly, the batteries still work. I brought it downstairs so we can listen to it while we get the café ready to reopen."

"Is there anyone here?" Stella was just about to tell the tall young man at the door that the café was closed, when Baz jumped up and held open the door.

"Dane! It's been too long." Baz turned to Stella. "Dane is Mae's cousin. He is our electrician."

"Baz! It has been too long. I bet you still make the best espresso in Brisbane! I wanted a job out this way, so I had an excuse to order some of your famous brew, but I didn't expect the job to be here. I heard you had a bit of bother." Dane grinned. "I have a new stove in the truck. We'll have the place up and running again in no time."

"And then I'll make you the best espresso ever!" Baz replied.

Stella and Baz left Dane to get the electrical work sorted. Stella wasn't sure whether it was nervous energy, or whether Baz was simply pleased to see Dane. He was certainly a lot happier today. Stella's stomach had stopped doing flip flops too. Physical activity, in this case cleaning up the mess, was easing Stella's anxiety.

"I'VE CHECKED AND REWIRED the electricals in the kitchen." Dane bounced through the swinging door. "The new stove, and oven are both in place and working. Keep the paperwork somewhere handy. In case anyone wants to check it." Stella opened the cupboard under the front counter and placed the papers Dane handed over straight into the folder that contained the police and fire report. Stella's obsessive compulsive tendencies acted in much the same way as anxiety or a stomachache. She took a slow breath, as she tucked the papers together. Knowing this at least was under control calmed her nerves. The faint ticking as her blood circulated through her body. An awareness of her body became stronger the more she tuned in to her supernatural abilities.

"I also checked the structural integrity of the building. I happen to be a licenced builder as well. Dad's fault, we're all high achievers, like he is. I mean he is a qualified electrician and a plumber in addition to being a builder and an architect. It runs in the family." He grinned. "I have signed off that the building is structurally safe. No damage in that sense at all. I did replace some wood panelling, but mainly for aesthetics. For Mae. She likes everything just perfect, but you guys know that," he said with a wink at Baz. "The paperwork is in that bundle I just gave you."

Before Stella could respond, she saw Flix tapping on the kitchen window. "That's great Dane. Thanks so much for your help today. It's such a relief to know that there wasn't too much damage. A quick coat of paint and we'll be ready to open for business. Why don't you two go and grab an early lunch?" she suggested. "I'm going to double check we reordered all the food to replace what we had to throw out, due to fire, smoke, or water damage. Can you bring me a cuppa and something with chocolate?"

Both men grinned at Stella. They left the café chatting animatedly, old friends who hadn't seen each other for ages. She shut the door behind them before heading out the back door to see what Flix wanted.

Brigid stood at the door. Stella felt her heart sink to her toes. Embracing her friend she asked, "Is everyone okay? What are you doing here?"

"Thanks a lot," Brigid countered dryly.

"I didn't mean it like that. It is wonderful to see you. It's just that I haven't seen you travel anywhere before. For you to use a portal now, whatever is going on must be serious. Come and sit down." Stella ushered her to a table in the café, double checking that she had locked the front door.

"I don't normally travel. To be honest I don't like it much. I end up feeling seasick. But I had to come and see you. In our realm people are getting sick and I thought you might be able to help. They are waking up with rashes, incredibly itchy red blotches everywhere. It is worse when they go outside in the sun. Some people are scratching themselves so much they are bleeding. We thought you might have something in your apothecary that could help."

"Something similar is happening here. I think it has to do with whatever is going on in the realm. I wish I was there with you; I am sure we could work it out together." Stella felt Brigid's frustration and didn't want to add to it. "There will be plenty of time for us to get together and create magic. In my apothecary, the back wall has the potions stored by the ailments that they are used for. You want the skin allergies section. Try the aloe, the chamomile and calendula. Lavender too if needed. Make poultices and layer on the sores. Keep the patients as still as possible and out of the sun for as long as you can. Once we ease their symptoms, we will need to determine what is causing the allergy. For now, though, the focus is on making people feel more comfortable." Stella reached out and took Brigid's hand. "Will you and Maisie be able to handle that? I mean you both have your businesses to run too."

"We are more worried about our customers than our businesses. Other people are helping as well." Brigid squeezed her hand back. "I know you want to help us, but I think you have to stay here for now."

"I agree. I will pay more attention to what is happening here, and on finding the cause. I suspect that if we can find the cause of the allergy here, we will find the cause of the allergy in your realm too." Stella squeezed her friend's hand. "It is so good to see you, Brigid. I'll be back home soon. As soon as I can."

"I know that. I keep telling Maisie that you'll be back in no time. Yet still she worries about you."

"Well now you'll be able to tell her that you have seen me and that I am perfectly fine. That there is no need to worry about me. If she knows that we had a fire here, please tell her it is all sorted, and no one was hurt. When she finds out we are also experiencing an outbreak of allergies, can you make sure she understands that in our world we have medical knowledge and experience dealing with illnesses. People generally don't get as sick here as in your realm. When I work out the significance of the laundrette, I'll let you know." Stella paused, then asked, "Where is the portal that bought you here? I haven't found one here yet. Although I think that door at the laundrette is one." Stella was curious how her friend had managed to visit.

"I didn't use a portal. Broomhilda helped me travel through my dreams. She is with Maisie while I am here. I volunteered to visit to ask you about how we could help those afflicted." Brigid stood up. "I had better get back."

"Stay safe, the both of you. I love you ladies." Stella watched Brigid leave through the back door of the café.

"Who were you talking to?' Baz handed Stella a cup and a chocolate muffin.

"Yum! Thanks. My friend Brigid." Stella preferred to tell the truth as much as possible. Trying to remember fibs she had to use caused the blood vessel responsible for migraines to start throbbing. "She heard about the fire, and she came to check on me. She left through the back. It is a quicker way to get back to her work." Noticing that Baz was by himself, she asked, "Where's Dane? And how did you get in? I know I checked the front door was locked."

"He had another job he had to get to. He promised to call in one day for that expresso. Dane had Mae's key, he let me in when we realised it was locked. I called into the hardware shop on the way back. Doug's mixing up the paint we need, and he'll deliver it here in a about half an hour. It won't take long to get that wall patched up and painted. We should be able to open for business again first thing tomorrow morning. If we can get everything else sorted this afternoon," Baz added.

"Yay!" Stella put down her cup and gave Baz a hug. "That's amazing news. Mae will be pleased. Can you let her know? She'll be expecting to hear from us, unless Dane has already given her the good news. I'm going to confirm with our supplier that they received the order I sent through first thing this morning, and what time they're planning to deliver. We should double check that we have everything we need, and that everything we use, is clean and in good condition." She paused, wondering if there was anything else they needed to do.

"I BET YOU WERE BOSSY as a kid too," Baz said with a laugh.

EXHAUSTED BUT PLEASED that the café would be busy again tomorrow, Stella climbed the stairs to her flat. She was optimistic that she and her friends would solve the mystery of the strange allergy that was affecting so many. The throbbing migraine across her left temple wasn't easing. Stella knew that too much caffeine and chocolate contributed to her affliction. She knew instinctively that if she drank a litre of water it would ease. Water, then research on the current health crisis. Mae had sent her laptop into the café with Dane. It made it easier for Stella to keep on top of the ordering and other admin at the café while Mae was still caring for her mother. The laptop would be handy to read up on the news about this latest outbreak. Further investigation at the laundrette would have to wait.

As soon as she opened the door to her flat, she sensed that something was different. Immediately she saw her *Book of Spells* was sitting on the table. Next to it were two small leather pouches. She opened one containing a rose quartz, an amethyst, and a clear quartz. The other contained lavender, rosemary and mugwort. She instantly recognised all the items. The last time she used them she was sitting in her apothecary. The collection of three items sitting out on her table meant one thing only. Magic. Someone wanted to help her solve the mystery of the newest viral allergy outbreak.

Stella flipped through the book, reading the spells she knew so well. Casting a circle, protection, the energy ball, and many others. The pages at the back of the book, Stella didn't recognise.

"Flix, I need your help," she called out, the sprite flew over and landed on the table, almost before she had finished speaking.

"What's up?" he asked glancing curiously at the book and the pouches, "That's new."

"I guess Brigid didn't bring these items with her. Did you happen to notice who or how these items appeared on the table?" Stella asked. Flix shook his head.

"I was here all day, except when I was helping Brigid and Broomhilda. Oh my, what if these are booby trapped and something happens to you?" Flix, jumped up, inspecting the items closely.

"I don't think they are dangerous." Stella calmed the sprite down. "Since discovering I have magical abilities, I receive things—gifts—from time to time. I told you that my coat pockets often hold unusual items that are just what I need at the time?" Flix nodded and Stella continued, "Well this book has just appeared when I needed it, on more than one occasion." She shrugged. "I know I'm not supposed to be doing any magic at the moment. I suspect Kai and whoever she is working for knows that I have been using my powers. As much as I want to find that portal in the laundrette, I promised Brigid I would try to find the source of the health crisis here and across the realm. So now I've been given these tools and I'm pretty sure that means I'm supposed to be doing something with them. What do you think?"

Flix looked at the book, the pouch of herbs and the crystals. "I think you're right," he said cautiously. "I can't sense any dark magic attached to them. I am confident you will work out to do to resolve the challenges we are facing in both realms. I will let Broomhilda know you have these tools, and I will let you know what she says."

As Flix jumped down, to seek advice from the oldest fairy in the realm, Stella closed her eyes. She flipped through the book until her intuition screamed *Stop*!

THE BOOK LAY OPEN AT one of the new pages that Stella hadn't seen before. The Eye of Horus—a sign of prosperity and protection that dated back thousands of years to ancient Egypt. The incantation below it spoke of cleansing a world polluted with toxins. Toxins and chemicals created a barrier to focus and understanding. People became distracted and focused only on themselves. Consumed with negative emotions. The downwards spiral into depression became as contagious as the original contagion.

Stella closed her eyes and flipped to the next page. Squeezing them tight to block out the image. Curious, she opened them again. The illustration of the skin infection was gross enough. The explanation, that an outbreak of this kind could be caused by the mere wave of a wand and a specific incantation, was horrifying. Magicians with evil intent could cause a large group of people to experience the same symptoms. Such as an outbreak of skin allergies. Left untreated meant the toxins went on to trigger depression, and other negative emotions. This could result in disaster, in both realms.

Turning back to the previous page Stella's stomach clenched with anger. How dare someone mess with people's health and free will? She was doubtful that the solution would be as easy as speaking aloud the Eye of Horus incantation. This ancient rite must be performed during a specific moon phase. A coven, or group of people with pure intent, to heal without any benefit to themselves must be present. Stella mulled over this information for a while. Instinct told her not to bother Broomhilda or the others until she had all the facts.

"I have found some information," she told Flix. "It is only the start of what I need to learn. In this realm it isn't as easy as setting up my apothecary as I did with Brigid and Maisie. No matter how bad it gets here, I don't think the general public are ready for witchy healing practices."

"Broomhilda suggested you try to get a good night's sleep. She has the feeling that tomorrow may provide some answers, and more questions."

"DID YOU KNOW THERE were customers lined up, before you opened this morning?" Mabel smiled at Stella, placing her order for a small espresso and a piece of carrot cake. "I was taking my cat for a walk around five thirty."

Stella smiled back. "Yes, we actually opened a little earlier than normal when we realised that people were waiting for the café to open."

"I admire your energy and your motivation. You must be a very organised person, getting everything up and running so soon after the fire," Mabel gushed. Stella still couldn't work out if she should be worried about this super friendly lady, or simply enjoy the conversation.

Handing Mabel her order, Stella smiled, deciding to give her the benefit of the doubt, "Have a great day."

There was a steady stream of people ordering their grand re-opening special of ten dollars for a coffee and cake combo; an idea Stella had raised with Mae late yesterday afternoon. Mae had expressed concern that after being shut a couple of days, there might be a lack of customers. Baz was happy to stay late and bake some delicious cakes, carrot, banana, orange and poppyseed and chocolate. She need not have worried about a lack of customers. Even with the news that more people were presenting to the doctors with allergies, orders for coffee, cakes, and sandwiches continued right through until early afternoon.

Everyone knew someone who was either in hospital or thinking of going to hospital with an allergic reaction to something. Rather than cautiously staying home, people seemed to need to socialise and talk about what was happening. An idea slowly bloomed in Stella's consciousness. This time the pounding in her head was connected to her magic. Stella could feel the difference; this was energising and not exhausting. The idea was more than a little unconventional, but it just might work.

"I heard you've both done an amazing job getting the café up and running," Mae said, when she popped in after lunch. Baz beamed, cleaning the coffee machine in between customers.

"We did our best," Stella said. "Baz is fantastic at cleaning, talking to customers, and everything in general. You're very lucky he's part of the team. I did want to talk to you about something, if you have time." Stella hesitated at first but decided the best option was to barrel ahead.

Mae nodded. "Come and sit by me. I'm running errands while my sister spends time with Mum, so I do have some time." Mae sat down at the nearest booth. "I hope you aren't telling me that you're leaving, moving on to see more of our beautiful country. I don't think now is a particularly safe time to go travelling. The news is talking about thousands being affected by the virus now. They are calling it a virus rather than an allergy because it is affecting so many people. How crazy is that?"

Looking at her hands—healing hands—her inner voice prompted her to speak what was on her mind. Stella lifted her head, facing Mae. "Well, I have worked in alternative health care before. Using essential oils, herbs, and plants to help support our health. I believe that we can heal some things with certain foods and teas. Some foods make us sick; some can heal." Stella took a breath. She had forgotten how passionate she felt when she spoke about this. She felt her energy vibrating and wondered if others could sense this.

"The current health crisis, I'm not saying that I have the answers, but I think I can help." She paused, assessing Mae's reaction. She couldn't read her, so she kept talking. "What I'd love to do is to have herbal teas available here. Peppermint, chamomile, green tea, lemon and ginger. Nothing too outrageous." She resisted the urge to fiddle with the napkins or get up and clean something. *Calm. Breathe.*

Mae glanced at Baz, then looked directly at Stella. "I think that's a wonderful idea. I do have one question before I agree. How long are you planning to stay here with us?"

"I'm not sure yet." Stella decided honesty was the best option. "I've a few things I have to do in Brisbane before I continue with my trip. I don't know how long that will take. I think at least a couple more weeks. If I work out more details, I'll let you know."

"I appreciate you being truthful," Mae told Stella. "Our supplier does stock a range of herbal teas, so you can order through them. I was going to place an order in the next couple of days. Why don't you keep hold of my laptop and place an order for the teas you think might work here?"

SCROLLING THROUGH THE products available on the website, Stella ordered a selection of teas, and made note of some of the other items they had available. The company had a range of healthy options; some of them might be useful in the future.

Baz sat next to Stella. The spicy scent of ginger wafting in from the kitchen and the plate he placed in front of her. "Would you mind tasting my new creation?" he asked eagerly.

The ginger slice melted in her mouth. A faint taste of lemon and cinnamon mixed with the ginger invoked images of gingerbread men. "This is delicious."

"You inspired me. I heard you talking to Mae about healthy teas and foods. Mum taught me all about foods that heal. We used to cook for the oldies in our community. I thought we could promote our healthy food options here in the cafe."

"What a terrific idea Baz. Let's discuss it some more tomorrow. We might be able to plan a menu to offer to Mae. Right now, though, I think it's time we went home. It's been a big day."

FEELING BRAVE AFTER the conversation with Mae, Stella wondered if it was time to go back to the laundrette. Her energy was buzzing, it felt like a swarm of bees in her head. A brisk walk would help clear her head. "Any more dramas?" Flix questioned her as soon as she entered the flat.

"Thankfully everything in the café is back to normal," she replied. "That's one less issue to worry about. Is there any news from Broomhilda?"

"The herbs you suggested are working to a degree. It's easing the symptoms. We are no wiser as to the cause of the outbreak, although those wands you found are likely to be at the heart of it. Broomhilda wanted you to know that returning them was the right thing to do. Whoever is behind this, whatever this is, would have found another way."

A side effect of her powers was the ability to push through her fear and face whatever was next. Stella had not shared how she felt, with anyone. When her children were taken from her, Stella froze with fear, powerless to resolve the situation. Her stomach retched now, recalling those events only a few years ago. She swallowed hard, the lump in her throat refusing to budge. No time to ponder why that happened, or how she could have reacted differently. What motivated Stella now, drove her to find a solution, was anger. Anger that any individual or group of people could wield such power over others, causing illness, fear and pain.

"I don't know why I'm the key to this, but somehow I am," she told Flix. "I was taken from the realm and dumped here. They obviously thought I would be so occupied with getting home that I wouldn't be a threat. But why? What do I know?" Stella rubbed her forehead, activating her third eye. "I'm certain that the answers are close. The laundrette, the hooded figure, the fire, the outbreak, it is all connected. "Brigid bravely travelled here. Conquering her fear, for the sake of the people in her realm. We found the wands and are aware they contributed to the problems. My *Book of Spells* arrived with new pages that contain useful information. The herbs and crystals that arrived must be significant too. I know we agreed it was better that I don't perform any magic, but I want to try something."

"What exactly do you want to try?" Flix asked. "We don't know how the fire started, or what is going on at the laundrette."

Flix had a point. Stella groaned, her third eye stung, like when she accidentally got shampoo in her eyes. She closed her eyes for a second, opening them again quickly hoping that Flix wouldn't notice. By the worried look on his face she knew she hadn't got away with it. "I was just closing my third eye. Because I haven't been practising my magic, it is a little rusty. I will activate it a little later. Which kind of proves my point. I do need to perform a certain amount of magic, to make sure it will work if we do need to." She thought for a second. "It also proves your point, of caution, until we learn more."

Flix nodded approvingly. He wasn't going to like what Stella was about to suggest. "It would help if we knew what was on the other side of that door. My instinct tells me we do need to find that piece of the puzzle at least." Stella cringed, preparing herself for Flix's comment.

"When I spoke to Broomhilda she agreed with your theory that if you received the *Book of Spells,* the herbs, and the crystals, then yes you should be safe to use those tools. I reluctantly agree that we do need to follow your intuition. Please be careful. If it is a portal, I can't pass through it with you. Fairies and sprites can get caught and spun around and end up somewhere quite nasty unless we open the portal ourselves. That isn't one of my skills. I can see you, watch your journey from here, and protect you as best I can."

THE CLOCK ON THE TOP of the post office informed Stella it was a little after six pm. The laundrette was empty. Ignoring the part of her brain screaming that this was not a good idea, she walked past the machines and opened the back door. With no plan as to what she was going to do when she ended up somewhere strange, she landed with a thud.

Stonehenge.

The ancient monument welcomed her as it always did. Her energy beat in rhythm with the primal Celtic magic infused in the stones. Stella skin prickled as the hairs on her arms stretched out towards the pull of the ancient enchantment. There was something odd about this visit, and not because she had just walked through a portal. It wasn't because it was a different time of day to her visit to Stonehenge at sunrise on midsummer morning last year, as the winner of a competition. Recalling the energy and emotions of that glorious sunrise sent shivers along her spine. Coincidentally the visit had allowed her to work with her newly discovered coven, to close some portals and save the world. Just the thought of what she achieved sent her pulse racing.

"So, this is what it looks like at the end of the day," she whispered as the sun slowly sank behind the horizon, emitting an eerie glow across the land. Her fingers felt something, hard and smooth in her coat pocket. The moonstone she found began to vibrate in the soft moonlight. Mesmerised by the shimmering stone and the feel of its frequency in the palm of her hand. Stella closed her left hand over the stone. She placed both her hands firmly back in her pockets.

Returning her attention to the magnificent structure, she stepped back, studying the area around the stones. Stella sensed that she was viewing the stones in the time she shared with Brigid and Maisie. There was a stillness in the air that was lost in the modern-day hustle and bustle. The air felt different when she travelled through time. Simpler, cleaner, uncorrupted electrical currents, technology, metal, and concrete.

I know what's missing. She squinted in the direction of the road that ran past the ancient stones. Six months ago, there was a main road with a constant line of traffic. Now there was no road and no cars. Moving closer to the stones, she found other subtle differences. The guides had described visitors cutting away pieces of the stones, marking them with lipstick and paint. Lichen grew on some of areas where the paint had remained. None of this was evident in this earlier version of the structure.

The sky darkened with each minute that passed. There was an unnatural purple hue to the sky, darker in the east, lighter in the west as the sun sank below the horizon. As Stella scanned the horizon, she noticed a slow moving bright reddish light. It appeared to be moving towards her. Mesmerised by the brightness and vibrancy of the colour. After a few seconds Stella figured out what she was looking at. She gasped.

Hundreds of people with torches marching along in a line, the flames glowing red as they moved towards her. *Towards Stonehenge.* The only place to hide was behind the imposing stones. Closer and closer the red mass came towards her. She could hear the chanting, the noise of hundreds of people all marching in tune to their own sombre monotone chant.

The stone was cold against her face. She leaned in, pressing herself as close to the outermost stone as she could. Crouching, willing herself to disappear, her eyes fixed on the red glow. Were there other armies marching in around her? In a panic she scanned the entire landscape. A huge sigh escaped her. No other armies were headed towards Stonehenge. Slight, subtle movement, like the flutter of Broomhilda's wings caught her eye.

She would welcome Broomhilda, or any of her clan, should they appear now. Part of her wanted to see what was going to happen when the group reached the stones, and part of her wanted to be anywhere else.

Slowing her breathing, with her fingers on the crystal in her pocket. Suddenly she knew exactly what she had to do. Stella stood up. Holding her hand out in front she called to her golden ball of energy. She knew that some of the approaching group may notice the glow of her energy. She counted on the fact that she would be able to quickly activate her invisibility cloak. The familiar golden orb pulsating between her outstretched hands grew bigger as it joined with the ageless magic of this land. Her energy grew stronger. In the flat she tried to use her magic un-noticed, this time she didn't try to hide. Her energy grew until the glow nearly out shone the crowd in front of her.

Without warning all the light disappeared. Stella checked her body, making sure she was in one piece. *What just happened?* She seemed okay and she felt the safety of her cloak around her. She was confident she had successfully invoked her cloak. Surveying the area ahead where the crowd had been fast approaching, she blinked and rubbed her eyes.

They were gone. Every last one of them. Not one flame remained. Not one person or any evidence that there had been any people marching towards Stonehenge. The sky was dark and heavy. The purple hue had a menacing feel about it.

Intuitively she felt the fae behind her. Their agitation was evident. Just as surprised as she was that a line of over a hundred people had suddenly vanished. Stella wasn't sure if she should turn around and identify herself and try to find Brigid and Maisie or figure out a way to get back to Brisbane.

The decision was made for her when she heard women's voices behind her. She swung around, holding her breath. She was fearful that they may be able to see through cloak. Two hooded women, whether they were the same women who hid the package in the machine at the laundrette, Stella couldn't be certain. Heads huddled together as they muttered words Stella couldn't quite catch. Satisfied they could not see or sense her she waited to see what would happen next.

"So where are they?" Blondie asked. "They are supposed to be here by now. Typical! I should have organised this myself. It is the laundrette all over again."

"Hey, we did get the wands back." The woman with darker hair defended herself. "Cleo said they were definitely on their way."

"So where are they then?" demanded Blondie. "One hundred people don't just disappear. This is not acceptable! Wait, can you hear something? I swear I can feel someone, right here somewhere." She grabbed the air so close to Stella that she grabbed her cloak tight lest it should reveal her hiding place. "Something is wrong, I can feel it."

"I can feel the energy too, it is so innocent and good and positive—yuck!" Dark Hair shuddered. "We had better go." As abruptly as they arrived, the women walked through to the spot where Stella had closed the portal the year before.

Like watching a scene from a movie on a screen, Stella saw the women talking to another lady. Inching closer to try to hear what they were saying, moving quietly so they wouldn't feel her energy. The only words she could make out were, *health crisis, control, takeover* and *gold.* A wave of nausea spread over her as a foreboding negative energy cloaked her, enveloping her like a thick smelly musty blanket. Stella closed her eyes as her legs crumpled beneath her. *Is this what it feels like to faint?*

"WE HAVE TO HURRY." Luna handed a crate full of jars to Catherine, and one to Tizzie. "Brigid, Maisie, you watched how we created those salves, do you think you can replicate that in Stella's apothecary?"

The pressure in Stella's ears was overwhelming. Disoriented she remembered to yawn, as that had relieved the pressure when she travelled in a plane or was suffering the flu.

She could hear her friend's voices. They were muffled as if she was listening to them through a tunnel. Her eyelids were heavy, it took a few seconds to properly open her eyes, and a few more seconds to work out where she was. Stella recognised the workshop where she had first met Luna's coven. She opened her mouth to speak but no words came. No sound escaped from her mouth. As she tried to catch Brigid's attention, she realised it was like she was watching from behind a glass, although there was no glass there. Frantic energy welled up just beneath the surface, her whole body switched to panic mode. *I should close my eyes again. It is probably just a bad dream, and I am tucked up safely in bed.* The knot of panic that was gripping her chest gradually faded as she focused on slowing her breathing. Stella felt calmer. She could hear snippets of the conversation.

"Illness and allergies are a distraction. People will become too weak to think," Luna whispered. "That's what the radicals want. They want to slowly take all the magic in the realm and use it for themselves. If they confuse us so that we are running in circles too exhausted to think clearly or realise what is going on around us, they will win."

Stella kept her eyes closed, focusing on the words.

"For their plan to work the spell must be complete before the first quarter moon has passed. If they stop us from making decisions and taking action, it's easier to take our magic," Catherine whispered back.

"Gold, frankincense, myrrh cure allergies." the voices faded away.

Stella opened her eyes. Home. Her apothecary looked the same as the last time she had entered those doors, with the travellers. A wave of relief swept over her. The shelves she had spent hours cleaning and tidying stood tall and reassuring. Jars of herbs and potions glistened in the moonlight shining through the window near the front door. Made of an ancient wood, the work bench in the middle of the room was Stella's favourite piece of furniture. The bench had belonged to Luna and other garden witches before her. She donated it to Stella when she took on the apothecary.

A book lay open on the work bench. She didn't recognise that version of the *Book of Spells*. Maybe Maisie or Brigid left their copy there, to work on a cure for the allergies? Brigid and Maisie had shown Stella how to manipulate the elements, she had taught them herbal medicine and how to use portals. Broomhilda had cautioned against leaving the sacred book out where others could see it. Magic was memory and intuition as much as written word or teaching.

Her friends were huddled together over the cauldron, measuring ingredients. They weren't directly referring to the open book. Stella squinted in an attempt to see the ingredients they were holding. She tried to stand and call out to them. Her legs again crumpled beneath her.

Plants that harm. Plants that heal. Herbs, and vegetables and fruit. Fresh foods, straight from the earth. Harvesting plants and preparing foods for shared meals. Using a mortar and pestle and blending herbs, roots, leaves, seeds, and flowers.

The natural world. Balance and harmony to heal and balance our world. We don't need to create something new, rather we embrace the old ways. What worked for centuries. Honest, caring, healing knowledge passed through families, through generations.

Fae Magic

S tella

Stella opened her eyes. She groaned inwardly. Another dark alley. She really needed to work on her transportation skills. She gingerly checked for injuries. The only evidence of her heavy landing was a bruise forming on her left thigh.

"Shh," a little voice whispered fiercely. "If you can walk, let's get home. This place gives me the jitters." Flix said.

"That's a good idea. Were you here the whole time I was gone?" Stella asked, tentatively putting weight on her left foot. She was thankful that apart from the thumping of a pressure ache at the bridge of her nose she was unscathed from her adventures.

"I sure was. Broomhilda's instructions were to keep an eye on you." Flix held up a mirror. "I could see everything." He returned the magic piece of glass to the pocket of his shirt. "You opened the door of the laundrette and fell through into Stonehenge. Stonehenge as it was centuries ago. The glow and energetic force you called on when you put on your invisibility cloak was felt throughout the realms."

"Oops. I was so worried that I would be seen. I didn't consider my magic would have such an effect." Stella considered this information. Her energy rippling through several realities and timelines was a sobering thought. "What happened to the group of people with torches and flames? Hundreds of them that were marching on Stonehenge. They all disappeared when I felt my cloak land to protect me. I didn't make them disappear, did I?"

"We don't think you did, but this is where our information becomes a little hazy." continued Flix. "But we do know there is a large coven, whose aim is to cause illness and confusion. To capture magic and use it for themselves, to gain more power. We have yet to figure out if they have a specific goal other than power and probably wealth. Stonehenge is a source of ancient power and mystery. They were likely trying to harness that power to complete their spell. Broomhilda thinks that maybe the force of your energy scattered the group, back to where they came from."

"Was Broomhilda there? I thought I felt the energy of the fae." Climbing the stairs to the flat Stella could feel her muscles tighten. Another side effect of travelling through the realms.

"She was at Stonehenge following the group of witches marching on the ancient stones. She felt your magic as you cloaked yourself," Flix replied. "She saw the women come through the portal and their reaction when the crowd disappeared. Broomhilda recognised one of the women as part of a coven whose sole purpose appears to be causing chaos and disruption."

"I saw them talking to a lady through a portal or a mirror. I didn't realise I could see through a portal to whoever was on the other side. Then something happened, maybe I fainted. I could see Maisie, Brigid, Luna and the others making remedies. I heard some of what they said, but not all of it. They couldn't see or hear me at all." Stella looked around her flat, relieved that there were no apparent signs that anyone had been there in her absence. "I don't know how I ended up back in the alley."

"When you disappeared from the stones, I couldn't find you. Whatever dark magic is in play it is messing with everyone's abilities. Neither Broomhilda nor I could get to you at first. When Broomhilda discovered you with your friends, she noticed something wasn't right. She decided we should bring you back here. She created the portal making it possible for us to drag you back through. We ended up in the alley. You woke up a few seconds after Broomhilda left to update your friends."

"The alley you dragged me to, is where I found myself when I landed in Brisbane the first time. Why are the portals behaving differently here? Are some portals for one way travel only?" Stella paused, seeing daylight sneaking in though the gap in the curtains that didn't quite cover the window. "Daylight? It is morning already? How long was I away?" Stella sat heavily on the kitchen chair. She winced as her bruise reminded her it wasn't her first heavy landing recently. Her legs were behaving oddly, feeling like jelly. Another side effect of the travel this time?

"Whoa, so many questions." Flix hopped up on the table. "Let me see if I can do this." Flix murmured some words that were indistinguishable to Stella. A plate with a piece of cake and a cup of tea appeared in front of Stella. "I don't normally perform such magic. But you need something to balance your energy. I am guessing you will be going to work and not spending the day catching up on your sleep.

Stella nodded, taking a sip of tea. The sweet, warm cinnamon flavour instantly bonded with her energy. The wave of heat loosening her tight muscles. She wriggled her toes feeling the liquid seeping into every part of her body. She felt Flix's eyes on her.

"You can feel it working. Good. Eat your cake too and I will answer your questions." Flix waited while Stella put a tiny piece of the cake in her mouth before continuing. "The portals are behaving differently since you arrived here. It's part of the spell the coven is weaving to distract those with abilities. If we are feeling sick, unwell, unenergized and the portals aren't reliable they can wreak havoc. That is one theory. You were gone all night. Time works differently at the moment. The same reason as the problems with the portals." Flix stood up. "Finish your food." He hopped down from the table, alighting on the window in a single fluid movement.

The magic of the fae was an ancient healing energy, intrinsically linked to nature. Stella remembered reading about it in one of Maisie's books. The cake tasted of citrus and mint, cardamon and chamomile. With each mouthful her pain eased. No more throbbing behind her eyes. Her limbs stopped aching. She sipped her cinnamon tea, infused with rosemary and lavender. The thin lace curtain that had been drawn over her third eye and brain, was now being dissolved. A gasp escaped her lips.

"Ah it's working I see." Flix turned from his position on the windowsill. "How are you feeling?"

Stella considered the question. She moved her neck to her left, then her right. Her shoulders next, then her arms. "I feel as if the tea has seeped into my cells, the core of my body and my mind. The cake has provided sustenance and energy. More alive, clearer, and more focused. Like fog has been lifted. Wide awake and full of energy." She took a breath to calm her excitement at how alive she was feeling. "Thank you Flix."

AS SHE LET THE WATER cascade over her in the shower, Stella sensed her energy flowing more calmly, as it had before she found herself in Brisbane. She felt her energy ebb and flow, a tingling sensation as if butterfly wings were fluttering around her. Behind her closed eyelids she sensed the heat of her energy between her palms. Mimicking a stream quietly bubbling along the countryside instead of a fully raging river, the power within her followed her lead.

Throughout the dramatic events of the previous twelve hours, her energy had raced to match her emotions. A marathon akin to racing from the top of the mountain to the bottom of the steepest gully in the snowy mountains.

Dressed and ready for work, she was grateful to be back in the relative safety of the flat. Her pen raced across the page as she jotted down everything she remembered from the previous night.

Purple sky—Stonehenge from centuries ago.

A long line of people with fire torches—disappeared when I used my golden ball energy.

Three women—two from the laundrette? One on the other side of another portal.

My energy was stronger, firmer, and lasted longer.

The feeling of fainting and watching the others in their workshops, but not being able to interact with them. It felt like she was being held under an old musty blanket which was somehow blocking my energy.

Brigid, Maisie, Luna, Catherine and Tizzie had worked out a cure, to the allergies, something about power ...

Once, Stella would have thrown down her pen in frustration at not being able to remember everything she saw and felt. Her intuition reminded her to stay calm this morning. Her inner voice often suggested she apply her patience and channel the serenity and elegance of the women from centuries ago. She decided to listen to their wisdom.

"Flix," she whispered, as the sprite obligingly appeared in front of her. "I am going downstairs. It is nearly time to open the café. Are you able to check with Broomhilda, to make sure Maisie and Brigid aren't in any trouble? The army of people marching on Stonehenge, their aura collectively was anger. They were aiming to start a fight or a riot. We don't know where they disappeared to. I am hoping that my coven and Luna's coven are safe and far away from any harm. Can you find out far the allergy has spread? Does Broomhilda know what has caused the sickness and what the cure is? She might have additional details." Stella took a breath before continuing. "I have a feeling that I know a lot more about last night than I can remember. I am not worried about that now; I am sure I will be able to fill in the gaps after some more coffee."

Flix rolled his eyes in mock horror, "Not more coffee!"

Stella smiled at the sprite. "I want to message my girls to make sure they are fine in the UK. I wouldn't mind hearing the radio news this morning, if there is any update this morning about the outbreak in Australia. I plan on going back into the laundrette, but under my invisibility cloak, after work tonight. Plus, I want to talk to Brigid and Maisie, and Luna."

"I can talk to Broomhilda while you are at work. I will get as much information as I can about what is happening and tonight, we can work out next steps. Please come back here before you go to the laundrette."

"Thanks, Flix! I won't go to the laundrette without you." Stella gave the sprite an awkward pat on his shoulder with her finger. She was grateful for all he was doing to help in this odd situation. "Is that hooded figure still hanging around? What did she do during all the commotion last night?"

"She is still there, in the shadows most of the time. When you are at work she disappears somewhere, but she always comes back. I lost track of where she was last night. We were focused on what was happening with you. Why?" Flix scratched his head, looking worried.

"It's just a hunch I have. I'm not sure whether she's dangerous, or maybe she's on our side. I think I'm going to go and say hello. I still have a few minutes until I have to be at work. I'll make her a coffee at the café and take it out to her. You can come too or watch to make sure everything is okay." Stella hoped she sounded more confident than she felt.

Flix nodded agreement. "I can tell you have made up your mind, so I will keep watch. If anything feels off, use your magic, to keep a safe bubble around you. I don't think she would risk causing a scene, but just in case."

BAZ WAS ALREADY DOWNSTAIRS getting the kitchen ready for a busy day, humming as he polished already sparkling clean pots and pans. "Stella! You're early, I haven't made your coffee yet."

"Morning Baz. I noticed someone sleeping rough out the back of the car park. Do you mind if I make them a cuppa and a sandwich before I start work?" Stella dropped ten dollars on the bench. "That would cover a ham and cheese toastie and a small flat white, wouldn't it?"

"You're an amazing lady! Yes, go right ahead and when you come back, I'll have a surprise ready for your breakfast.

STELLA CROSSED THE car park armed with the coffee and sandwich. She walked quickly, so as not to lose her resolve. The woman in the hoodie was hurriedly rolling up what looked like a makeshift tent made from a tarpaulin, tucked as far out of the light as she could get. The sun was starting to peek its head above the horizon through the buildings and trees. There was nowhere for her to hide.

"Hi I'm Stella." She offered the hooded figure the cup of coffee and the toastie. "I thought it was time we met properly. The food and drink aren't poison or anything. I'm not going to hurt you. You must be cold and tired, spending so much time out here. Even though it's summer the nights can get chilly."

The figure stared at her for a few seconds. She moved a step closer to Stella. "I'm Kai. Thank you. A cup of coffee sounds amazing." The two women stood in silence, appraising each other. Kai quickly ate the sandwich and drank the coffee.

Breaking the silence, Stella took an educated guess. "I think someone is making you spy on me. I don't know why, except that for some reason my magic is important. For them it's necessary to have me out of the way, or too confused to use my magic properly." Stella watched Kai for cues that she was right. Kai's fingers clenched the coffee mug tightly, her eyes telling Stella to continue with her theory. "I think you too are here under duress. You work for someone who's threatening you in some way. You're cautiously looking for a way out." Stella could see kindness in Kai's eyes, and a sadness she recognised all too well. Loss of a loved one, a family member, never fully heals.

Kai stood rigid, tears threatening to spill from her eyes. Stella sensed Kai was embarrassed and uncomfortable. Not wanting to alienate her, she said impulsively, "I think we could become friends. Good friends. We are both here, not of our own free will. We are both trying to make the best of a bad situation. I don't think that you want to cause me any harm. I think we should put our heads together and see if we can find a way out of this predicament for both of us. I must go to work now, but why don't you call in to the café later and we can have a cuppa and a chat?"

Kai nodded. The movement so small, Stella wasn't sure if she had misread it or not. "Hopefully we can catch up later. Have a good day, Kai." Stella concentrated on her steps. She focused on keeping her energy rhythm in tune with her breathing. Entering the café her fingers crossed that she had made the right decision.

Baz was deep in conversation with one of the regulars. It was just after six. Most of their customers would be on the train, or at home getting ready for their day. A line would soon form of people eager for their morning caffeine hit. The aroma of freshly brewed coffee with a hint of chocolate reached Stella. Her nose twitched. She glanced at Baz. His nod an indication that the mocha and banana bread was hers. Stella gratefully sat at the table closest the counter. Her stomach reminded her she had not eaten for nearly twenty hours.

Savouring the comforting warmth of the hot beverage, Stella wondered what her next move would be. Her heart yearned to be with Maisie and Brigid. It ached as she thought of her friends, and her family such a long way away. She was missing her kitten Puddles more than she thought she would. He was perfectly fine at her cottage in Canberra.

The idea of going home was almost too much to bear. She knew she had to be prepared to stay, at least for a while. Stella sighed inwardly. Her gift of second sight, that intuition that presented ideas and information to her so often was yelling that she had a job to do. Nibbling on the banana bread she smiled. There were benefits to having someone prepare her meals for her every day.

"You look deep in thought." Baz nudged her on his way back to the coffee machine. "Did it go all right outside?"

"Yes, she seems nice," Stella answered. "She might drop in later for a chat." she grinned at the expression on Baz's face. "She's okay. Like me, she's on holiday, camping out in unusual places while she travels. Me—I prefer home comforts—electricity and hot water et cetera. Which reminds me, if I'm going to stay here for a while, I really should buy some more clothes, and a phone charger."

"It'll be quiet in here for a while, after the lunch crowd. Why don't you pop out and get what you need then?" Baz suggested.

"Only if I get my chores done," Stella agreed. The jangling bell above the front door signalling the start of the morning rush.

"The news is crazy," Clint said chattily waiting for his long black and almond croissant. "More people in hospital with allergies, but only in Australia. The problem is, if they don't get it under control soon, all flights to and from Australia will likely be cancelled. Other countries won't want us Aussies travelling if we have some random virus or a mysterious allergy."

"I hope it doesn't come to that. I'm planning a visit to my children who are living in the UK," Stella commented, handing him his breakfast, and remembering her intention to message them earlier.

"I hope the government figures out the cause and the cure ASAP. People are freaking out about another pandemic. Scaremongers describing it as an air borne contagion of some kind. We didn't think it could get any crazier than 2020's pandemic." Clint waved his thanks as he left the cafe.

Remember. The whispered word as clear as if the being speaking was standing beside Stella. She hadn't heard that voice for a while. Last year she would often hear the whisperings of her ancestors and spirit guides. Encouraging her to follow her intuition and to practice her magic. The voices silent since her kidnapping. She welcomed their return.

But what did Stella have to remember? Was it too much to hope for a clue?

Remember. The voice was persistent.

A steady stream of customers throughout the morning kept Stella from thinking about that voice for a few hours. Many of the customers were taking their orders to go, rather than sitting and eating in the booths. Were they reluctant to stay out in public for long periods of time in case they caught the virus? The health scare was all over the media. Could it be a little quieter in the aftermath of the fire? It made the clean up after lunch a lot quicker.

"I've wiped down all the tables," Stella told Baz, placing some cups in the sink. "Do you need a hand cleaning up in here?"

"I have it all under control." He grinned. "Didn't you have a few errands to run?"

"Yes, thanks I'll duck out and get a couple of things. The thing is, if you notice my new friend come in, can you tell her that I'll be back later? I don't want to miss catching up with her."

"Of course! Now go, I've got this!" Baz flapped his tea towel at her.

FOLLOWING A HUNCH, Stella walked in the opposite direction to the laundrette. The tingling of her energy, like pinpricks on her skin, affirming she made the right decision. A convenience store, a chemist, a newsagent, and a couple more op shops. A Chinese takeaway, a fish and chip shop and a bakery. A sign pointed the direction of the train station on her right. Intrigued by the alleyway off to the left, Stella walked past *The Corner Pub*, an art studio and a clothing boutique.

The Crooked Cauldron. The black wrought iron sign on the post outside the door at the end of the alley was intriguing. Pushing open the door, Stella sensed the electric current of ancient magic woven into the very walls and furniture of the space. The atmosphere within the shop was as if she had stepped into a little shop in a back alley in London centuries ago.

"Can I help you with something?" an elderly lady appeared from behind a huge counter which was covered with crystals, tarot cards, feathers, and bundles of dried herbs.

"I'm not sure. I was just wandering around the area, and I found your store. It feels like I've been here before. You have some beautiful items," Stella said, admiring some of the crystals on the countertop.

"Do you like crystals, or maybe some cards?" the lady ran her long-nailed fingers lovingly across the items.

"I do love those crystals, and the tarot cards too." Stella acknowledged. "But I'm more interested in the dried herbs. Do you have any dried herb teas for memory and intuition?"

"Why yes I do, my dear." Indicating the far wall where bunches of herbs hung drying. Squinting at Stella she asked, "It does feel like I know you. Have we met before?"

Remember. Stella glanced at the shopkeeper to see if she had heard the word whispered less softly this time. There was no indication that she had heard any spirit words uttered with an urgency. Stella did wonder why it was up to her to solve this riddle. Surely there were others, like this witch behind the counter in a magic store, who were far more qualified.

"I think we might have met in a previous life," Stella said cautiously. "I have this habit of making connections with women from other places and times."

"Ah, now I remember where I know you from!" exclaimed the storekeeper. "You have been in Catherine's tavern. I am sure it was you."

Stella nodded, still not convinced she should say too much. This woman was either a threat or an ally. She was not yet sure which. "Possibly. I have been there, and other places too. How long have you had this shop here?"

"On and off for years. Before it was here it was somewhere else. As you know if you have crossed worlds, sometimes people and places move and appear in different parts of the realms. It doesn't always make sense at the time. My name is Mildred." She held her hand up in a flourish, the golden polish on her nails glistening, even in the muted light of the shop. Stella jumped involuntarily; the action reminded her of raising a magic wand. If Mildred noticed Stella's reaction, she didn't say anything. Which was fortunate as Stella herself couldn't work out why her body flinched. Another memory to access somehow.

On impulse, following her instincts, Stella asked the question that had been on the tip of her tongue since she entered the shop. "I'm Stella. Do you know of any magical activity or portals in the area? I am not a local, but due to unforeseen circumstances I will be staying here a while."

"Funny you should ask about magic and portals." Mildred motioned for Stella to sit down. Two patchwork chairs under a sign in flowery script that indicated this section of the shop was the reading corner. Mildred waited for Stella to choose a chair and then plopped herself down on the edge of the seat of the remaining chair. "In the last week I have seen more clients than I normally would at this time of year. Customers are buying divination tools, scrying tools, and crystal wands. People have been talking about a way to cross over realms. A door in the back of a shop. It isn't here, which people think is strange, being that this is a magic shop, of sorts. My coven has spoken about the laundrette as being the place to cross over into the other realm."

"It's true, I have seen it, and crossed through it." Excitement at finding Mildred and her store of magical mystical things gurgled through her veins. "I need to get back to work soon. Can we meet up again later? I would love to talk some more."

"Sure. Come back after work. I'll be here." Mildred handed Stella a packet of herbs. "These will work for increased memory and intuition. They are strong, so once a day only." Mildred waved Stella away when she tried to pay. "I get the feeling we will be kindred spirits. I am sure you will have the chance to help me one day."

Stopping at the first op shop, Stella found not one but three purple shirts, some denim leggings with butterflies, and brand-new packets of underwear. "I don't suppose you have any phone chargers?" she asked the volunteer sorting through the piles of clothes on the counter.

"We aren't allowed to sell electronic equipment, but if you want to have a look through that box of cables, you are welcome to take one if you find it," she responded.

"I KNOW I'M BACK LATER than I planned," Stella said as she dumped her bags in the back of the kitchen. She turned to Baz. "I can hold the fort if you want to go and run errands or anything."

"You're the first woman I have met who doesn't love spending hours shopping and buying things. I always spend ages picking out new clothes. Now, show me what you bought," he said enthusiastically.

"I found some really cool clothes at the op shop." She held up the shirts so Baz could see them. "And they even had a phone charger. They couldn't sell it to me, but I was welcome to take it to see if it works on my mobile." Stella didn't show Baz the herbs she got from Mildred. She wasn't sure how open he was to the mysteries and secrets of a world that wasn't based on logic. She couldn't wait to sample the herbs and see if they prompted her memory.

"I am guessing you like purple." Baz himself wore pink or flowered shirts under the long black apron. His pants either black or blue, depending on the day. "And you really weren't gone for very long at all.

The afternoon crowd should be here soon. I don't have anywhere else to be. I love it here. We meet so many interesting people."

Glancing at the clock, Stella was surprised to see she had been gone for less than an hour. She was certain she had been in conversation with Mildred for ages. In reality it mustn't have been very long at all. Was there magic in the store that somehow warped time, or made time move more slowly than normal? Stella had read about a spell that could morph time, so that the person could disappear to complete a task and return without being missed.

Remember. The voice started again.

The door opened, signalling the afternoon coffee rush. Everyone was talking about the allergy sweeping Australia.

"According to the latest news, the virus seems to target mostly the middle-aged—men and women. The opposite of who we normally identify as the most vulnerable people. There aren't many oldies or children presenting to hospitals with symptoms. At least that is what the reporters are telling us today. Tomorrow they might have more information." Chelsea from the chemist told the group waiting for their coffee.

"If it's an allergy, would taking antihistamines work?" Baz wondered aloud, to no one in particular, as he handed a large cappuccino to Dave from the hardware store.

"We don't know yet," Chelsea responded. "But for now, we're suggesting that's probably the best option. There may be other solutions. Our naturopath is looking into herbs and natural products – plants - that might help. Thanks for the coffee, Baz," she said as he handed her a small espresso.

"May I suggest that a herbal tea with stinging nettle and butterbur might help with the allergies?" Mildred came into the shop, quietly sitting at a corner booth just near the door. Citrus fruits, and foods high in vitamin C will also help. At least that's what I would try."

"Baz, this is my new friend Mildred. I visited her beautiful shop today. She's a herbalist. She knows her stuff when it comes to illnesses and curing them naturally." Stella turned to Mildred. "I'm so pleased you called in. What can I get you?"

"I can serve the rest of the customers, so you can sit a while with Mildred." Baz handed Stella two cups. One was the cup of black coffee Mildred ordered, the other a mocha. "Thank you," Stella said, making a mental note to find something special for Baz next time she visited shops. Three booths were occupied with customers enjoying a late afternoon coffee and cake. The special of the day was salted caramel mud cake with hot fudge sauce. Stella loved the tiny piece she tried when Baz had asked her to taste test it. She marvelled at how he had time to make such delicious cakes as well as the sandwiches and everything else he made each morning. It wouldn't take long to tidy up. Baz had cups for the remaining orders lined up on the counter. Stella sat down across the table from Mildred.

She took a sip of the mocha. "I've been thinking about the allergies that we're hearing about on the news, and I wonder, do you think it's linked to the opening of the portals? If there is a portal open here, then there are probably other portals opening around Australia," Stella mused aloud. "I think this virus was created by magic. Magic from far away, from one of the other realms. I think there is a group who wants to create confusion, and then take power from people for their own gains."

Mildred, watching Stella as she spoke, responded quietly, "I think you are right. I have been researching this as well. I remember most of my past lives, and I have been a herbalist in most of them. I've seen this type of illness before, created by malevolent beings set on destruction. Each time, there have been brave individuals who have fought against the evil and won. But still, people thirst for power and glory and decide to try to disrupt the balance of nature." Pausing, Mildred considered a moment before continuing, "Do you remember your past lives?"

Sipping her drink, Stella thought about how she was going to respond. She decided to follow her intuition and trust Mildred, to a point. "I don't really remember who I was in my previous existences, but when I travel through the portals, I recognise places and people. It is like the pieces of the jigsaw puzzle reveal themselves to me a piece at a time. The more I try to remember specifics, the less likely it is that I will gain insight at that particular moment. My intuition reminds me to be calm. At the same time, my spirit guides whisper the word *remember*."

"Do you remember, when you are prompted to by your guides?" Mildred asked.

"Not really. It's so frustrating. I'm certain that I'm here to help, that there is something I can do, to assist with solving the mystery of the illness, here and in the other realm. I'm slowly starting to piece it all together."

Mildred replied, "I sense things about people, like an empath, except that other secrets are revealed to me. For example, you have a complicated family story. You are far away from home; you have two places you call home. This place is temporary, necessary. Quite often it's like starting a painting and having no idea what it will look like when it's finished."

Mildred paused, and drained what was left of the coffee from her cup. "You often find yourself in the middle of a situation. The course of action you choose is to help other people. Your magic power is linked to your love of and understanding of plants that heal. Magic is bound to mysteries and secrets that reveal themselves in time."

The late afternoon caffeine cleared the remaining fog from Stella's brain. She wished her cup was bottomless. She could always have another, once the café was clean. "You're spot on with your assessment," she told Mildred. "I really should help Baz clean up. Thanks for calling in to the café. I'll visit the shop again tomorrow." Stella collected the cups on their table and those left behind by other patrons.

Baz had most of the kitchen clean already. It wouldn't take long to clean the remaining plates and cups.

"We're running low on some supplies." Baz placed the broom back in the corner behind the back door. "I've written a list for an online order. Do you mind watching the café while I grab some groceries? I don't want to run out of anything we might need."

Stacking the dirty dishes in the deep stainless-steel sink, Stella replied, "It won't take me long to wash these when you get back. I'll order the items online for you while you are out."

The bell above the door jangled as Stella finished ordering the foodstuff needed for the café. Kai walked in. "Is it too late for that chat?" she asked Stella.

"Absolutely not! Perfect timing in fact. I can practice making coffee and we can have a piece of his fabulous banana bread," Stella replied.

"You were right," Kai said, as they sat at the counter, each with a coffee and a piece of banana bread. "This bread is delicious! You were also correct this morning. I don't want to harm you. I work for a group of people, not from choice, but because of circumstances beyond my control. I'm hoping I can get free of their reach somehow. Earlier you spoke about working together. If you're still interested, I would like to help where I can."

"I'm definitely keen. My instincts tell me that we are supposed to work together to solve this. Are you from the other realm, or this one? And do you have any specific magical power? Oops sorry, that sounded nosier than I meant it to." Averting her eyes, she took a sip of her coffee, letting Kai decide what she wanted to share.

Baz waved from behind the counter. "I put away those groceries. Do you mind if I head home now? Everything is clean and tidy and ready for tomorrow. Just lock up when you ladies are finished."

"Thanks for today, and yes, go and I'll see you first thing in the morning. I ordered those groceries you wanted. They should be delivered tomorrow." Stella waved back. Turning to Kai, she added, "Don't think you have to leave. We can chat as long as we want to, and I'll lock up when we're ready to leave."

Kai spoke quietly, almost a whisper Stella leant close to hear her words. "I grew up in the other realm, born to a royal family well versed in the skills of magic and combat. As most teenagers do, I rebelled and came to Brisbane for a while. Denouncing my heritage. When I returned to the realm, I joined a coven. We helped people escape slavery, until I was captured and forced to work for a malevolent coven. It's the only way to keep my friends and other innocents safe, for now."

Sensing Kai was exhausted from sharing, and that there was still so much more to the story, Stella said, "Thank you for trusting me enough to share your story with me Kai. Do you want to hang around, maybe come upstairs or do you have somewhere you have to be?" Stella desperately wanted to visit the laundrette, but she wasn't sure if she should invite Kai along. She sensed Flix wouldn't be happy about that.

"You are very kind, Stella," Kai replied. "But not tonight. I know you probably want to visit that laundrette again, and to be honest I am curious about what will happen if you do."

Stella smiled. "I knew we were on the same wavelength. If I find a way to put a stop to the virus and whoever is causing the issues, would you work with me or would you have to take the other side?"

Kai shrugged. "A little of both, depending on how it pans out."

Our coven is our community. A group of beings who are of similar understanding of how the metaphysical world operates. As a group of people who trust and open ourselves up to the wonder and power of nature. We share ideas and knowledge in a community where we feel loved, and valued, respected simply for who we are and not for what we can do or what we bring to the group. Having said that, all members do bring valuable skills and knowledge. All people do have a piece of the puzzle and it is not by chance we meet those people who are in our lives. Sometimes our coven, our community is a group of people with whom we share a lifetime. Other times people come and go, as it is meant to be.

Remember

S tella

"Welcome home." Flix greeted Stella as she opened the door. "You had a busy day. Two new friends, what did I miss?"

"Kai is willing to help to solve the mystery illness, depending on what we find. She is being coerced into working for someone. She's looking for a way to win her freedom." Stella hung her new shirts onto the empty hangers in the cupboard in the bedroom. "She was honest. She wants to do the right thing. If she's made to work against us, we know it's because she doesn't have a choice. I'm hoping that we can discover a solution that will involve freeing her."

As she plugged in her phone charger, she remembered she wanted to text her girls. Within seconds she received a message confirming that they were fine. *"Sightseeing with the others."* Stella was glad the four of them were together and overseas, safe from the virus. A sigh of relief escaped her lips.

Remember. Whispered the voice.

"Okay, okay, I get it. Just let me make my cuppa and I will get right to it." Turning on the kettle for her herbal tea, ignoring the pang as she thought of the rift that still hung between her and her older two children. *Would she ever be able to raise the Christmas Curse, to enjoy the closeness, the relationship they shared before they were dragged away from her?*

"TALKING TO YOURSELF again?" Flix joked. "So do you want to know what I found out today?" The sprite jumped up onto the kitchen bench, sitting cross legged on the kitchen sink. "Ooh herbal tea! And it smells divine."

"I keep hearing the word, *remember*. I'm used to hearing voices, my spirit guides, or intuition or whatever you want to call them. This time it seems there is something I need to remember to help with the virus and everything else going on, here and in the other realm. I went for a walk today, and I found a herbalist. She gave me a packet of herbs to help with memory. I thought I would give it a try." Stella stirred in the herbs with the hot water, leaving it to steep before draining it.

"Sounds like a good idea. No doubt, that was the other lady I saw you talking to this afternoon. Did you check your coat pockets? Didn't you say that coat has a way of giving you what you need?" Flix inquired, cocking his head to one side.

"Flix you're a genius!" Stella said, grabbing her coat, she emptied the contents on the table. Three crystals, a couple of pouches of herbs, her notepad and pen, her wallet, and a piece of stone the size of her fingernail. She wouldn't have noticed it, it was so tiny, if it hadn't been vibrating and glowing.

The moonstone was smaller than a ten-cent piece. It was shaking the other crystals and items on the table with its energy. Stella passed her hand over the crystals, and they moved as if in unison under her spell. A tiny high-pitched bell like sound emanated from the crystals, blended with clinking sounds as they danced across the table.

"What the heck is that?" Stella glanced at Flix, who shrugged his shoulders. The sounds stopped as she moved the other items away from the crystals. Arranging the crystals into a circle with the moonstone in the middle, Stella again hovered her hand over the crystals, watching them dance and vibrate on the table, moving around until they were pointing in a straight line. Gradually the crystals slowed down until they all stopped moving. The moonstone was still lit up like it was holding sunlight, but it also slowed its vibration.

"If I take it that the moonstone is the tip of the arrow then it is pointing out the window. What direction is that?" she wondered aloud.

"East, I think," Flix piped up, stretching, and moving over to the windowsill. "The sun comes in here in the morning," he said helpfully. "Although a lot of things are also east. Shops, the coast and the beach if we go far enough. I am not sure that is helpful though. Let me go and check something out, I will be back later." Stella watched, admiring how nimble her friend was and how quickly he managed to disappear from her sight.

Straining the tea was proving difficult, without a tea strainer. "I don't suppose drinking any of the herbs will cause any issues, although I know that some herbs are poisonous." Taking a sip of the rose-coloured drink in front of her, she immediately felt a tingling sensation. Could the tea really be working so quickly?

"Did you miss me?" Flix grinned, startling her.

"I didn't expect you back so quickly." Stella took another sip of her tea.

"I just had to check; the laundrette is due east from here. I spoke to Broomhilda. Maisie and Brigid are busy helping people who are sick. Luna and her coven are working on finding a cure, rather than something that just calms the symptoms. None of them are sick, but they are so busy that they don't have time to look at the big picture." The sprite pulled out a tiny piece of paper from his pocket and referred to the words it contained. "It is almost certainly a curse on certain people, those with specific skills. The confusion and brain fog it is causing is worse than the skin allergies, but it is harder to diagnose, and resolve. Broomhilda thinks this is how the coven is planning to steal the magic."

"Broomhilda is open to you revisiting the laundrette. She agreed that as the new stone seems to be leading you there, that no harm will befall you there. On one condition. That I can ride in the pocket of your coat."

Stella's heart felt like it was going to pulse straight out of her chest. "Let's go!"

"What about your tea?" Flix pointed to the cup on the table.

Stella took another sip, savouring the taste, the warmth of the flavours and the buzz that resulted from each sip. "I'll reheat the rest of it when I get home," she said, gently lifting the sprite and placing him carefully in her right pocket. The tiny moonstone shimmering on the table caught her eye. "I'm going to take the tiny crystal too, in my other pocket," she said for Flix's benefit.

WALKING BRISKLY TOWARDS the laundrette, Stella was relieved to find it was open and empty. "More people must be staying home because of the virus scare," she whispered, marching over to the back door. "The handle is locked. I think I know how to open it with magic."

"Better not—" Flix started.

"Too late, it's open." Stella stared in awe at the ball of energy in her hand. Without concentrating on her powers, she had merely decided she wanted the door to open. Manipulating the elements to unlock a door was a new skill. Her hand tingled from the excitement of her accomplishment. Stepping over the threshold and closing the door behind her she kept her eyes open, prepared for the unexpected.

The now familiar ancient structure greeted them. The darkened sky held a few early evening stars, and a slight sliver of moon. The tall grey rocks cast ghostly shadows in the open paddock. Stella felt the familiar buzz of energy at being this close to the mystical formation. It took all her will power not to reach out and hug one of the rocks. She felt an affinity with those who built it, several centuries past. "Stonehenge in the seventeenth century." She lifted Flix out so he could see for himself.

"Now what?" Stella wondered aloud, looking around for a clue or a signal of what to do next.

"Check your left pocket," Flix suggested.

"Good idea." The stone vibrated as her fingers touched the stone. "Only the stone." Holding it up in the palm of her left hand, the tingling sensation was comforting. "I can do this," Stella muttered more to herself than to Flix. "There are portals all around this structure. I didn't realise that when I was here last year." Getting her bearings, she continued, "I can see the portal I closed last year, the main door between the worlds. Then there is the portal we came through. If those points are due east and due west, then there are likely another two, one due south and one due north. That window into another world. I thought it was near the eastern portal, but I was wrong. I think it may have been the northern portal, which should be over here." Stella moved carefully between the stones, placing the hand with the stone in front of her.

"What are you doing here?" A stern female voice caused Stella to jump, luckily her reflexes were good, and she caught the tiny crystal before it dropped onto the ground. She slipped it into her pocket, she hoped, without anyone else noticing her sleight of hand. She turned around.

"I am just sightseeing. I have already seen Stonehenge in the daylight, and I wanted to see what it was like at dusk," Stella ad-libbed.

"How did you get here?" The tall lady to whom the stern voice belonged; her dark hair tightly wrapped up in a ballerina bun asked just as loudly.

On a hunch, Stella responded simply, "Through the western portal." Hoping to have given enough information to stem any additional questions. Logically there would surely be lots of magical folk who make the pilgrimage to this ancient site. As long as there was no poster out with her face on it, and as long as this serious lady wasn't one of the coven who banished her to Brisbane in the first place. Stella couldn't be sure, but the lady wasn't one of the group that she had encountered the previous evening.

"Make sure you don't stay too long. There is a dangerous element about these days. It is not safe to be out after dark." Heading for the north portal the lady, appeared to have dismissed Stella as someone of no consequence.

Stella wanted to follow the lady through the north portal to see what was on the other side. "I don't want to attract any more attention to myself, otherwise I would follow her." Stella sighed. "I wonder if I could pop through the south portal for a quick look?" She whispered to Flix.

"Only for a few minutes, to see where it leads," Flix cautioned. Excited and a little scared, Stella turned and walked through the portal.

"Where are we?" Flix whispered, unable to see anything from the comparative safety of the pocket.

"In the laundrette," Stella responded, disappointed. "I think the portals must act as homing devices. They take us where we are meant to be. So, the one portal can take one person to Stonehenge, and another person to Brisbane. Either that or the coven who are creating havoc with illnesses have hijacked the portals somehow."

"At least we are safe." Flix stood up so he could see out of the pocket. "Can we go home now? My stomach flip flops every time I travel through portals."

"It has been a long day, let's go home." Stella agreed with Flix.

PICKING UP THE PEN and notepad, Stella doodled as she sipped her tea. The taste tingled on her tongue, the zing of the flavours awakening some far distant memories. She had added a little fresh hot water to the liquid that had steeped, strengthening the impact of the herbs.

The memories and words that hovered just of reach, were coming closer. She felt their whisperings, in the urge to draw.

Images of the moon, pentagrams, the sun, herbs and flowering plants flew from her hand through the pen onto the paper. An old stone building and an ancient site, similar to Stonehenge, but with some subtle differences appeared on the page. Stella didn't pause to review her handiwork, she let her brain and her hand get the images out without imposing her own interpretation.

She turned to a new page as words tumbled from her pen.

laundrette –portal – Stonehenge, herbs – memory, Moonstone – intuition, coven – wisdom, allergies – immune, magic – power, north – south – east, west

Connection between middle age and power. What benefit to making non magical people sick as well? Money and power. Money and power from Australia? Why only Australia? And magic and power from the other realm – who are they and what do they want the magic for? Also, if the portals change destination depending on the person, is this a portal thing or has someone changed the portal destination? For what reason?

Who are Cleo and Cyril? Are they connected with the laundrette? What about the wands I found, and the witches who have been using the portal in the laundrette? Are Mildred and Kai who they appear to be?

The moon phases too, are important. Magic spells must be completed by the end of the phase of the moon, or the magic won't work.

"Maybe I'll sleep on it." Stella yawned, gently placing the pen on top of the notepad. The pen needed a rest too, it had never written so many words in such a short time. Taking her cup to the sink, she checked on Flix. Her heart melted, he looked so cute, curled up on a cushion on the floor, sleeping soundly, probably for the first time in a week. Knowing that Kai wasn't the enemy meant that the sprite no longer needed to keep watch out the window all night. She had the feeling Flix would only need a short nap and that if she should wake during the night, she would find him keeping watch as she slept.

Feeling a little tipsy, like the herbal tea had been a shot of tequila, Stella hopped into bed. "I'm sure I'll figure this out soon," she mumbled, as she drifted off to sleep.

Waking up in the middle of a field, the moonlight illuminated the book sitting on her lap. A *Book of Spells*. The tiny moonstone was glowing in her right hand. Although it wasn't vibrating, or warm to touch. Picking up the piece of moonstone in her left hand, she marvelled at the light emanating from such a small rock. She closed her eyes. When she opened them again she found she was back at the familiar site.

Stonehenge.

Half a dozen women were wandering amongst the stones. All with long black hooded cloaks, hands tucked in their pockets. Sparks of lightning from a storm to the east caught her attention. The others were paying her no consideration. The storm didn't concern them either as they walked in between the rocks. Their lips moved, but no words were heard. Stella stood watching the women. Were they in a trance? If they knew each other, there was no acknowledgement as they passed by each other. Their movements seemed random, but Stella suspected there was a purpose to what she was witnessing. The silence was broken by the clap of thunder, followed a few seconds later by lightning. The light highlighted the beauty of the stones, undamaged by the graffiti, the paint and the lipstick that tourists would later mar the rocks surfaces with. Stones that had not been chipped away at for tokens and souvenirs.

As she watched the women movements, she counted five. Surely there were six when she arrived. Watching more closely she realised that only four women remained. A shudder ran down the length of her back as cold fingers, with sharp nails ran along her spine like they were playing on a chalk board.

Concentrate. Her eyes focused on each of the remaining women. Four became three as one walked through a gap between two of the tallest pillars. Keeping her eyes on that spot, taking a chance that each of the women were existing at the same section of the monument.

A heavy, cold, dark cloth fell from the rock onto her shoulders. She jumped, her heart pounding in her chest, little sparks of energy flew out of her fingertips involuntarily. She clasped her hand over her mouth, so no sound would escape.

The two remaining women walked through the portal together.

A thud in the middle of her back as a hand propelled Stella forward. She tried to move out of the way, twisting her body to see who was pushing her.

No one was there. Was the spirit of the stone driving Stella forward, towards the open doorway? The initial shock replaced with trust, Stella wasn't scared, the spirit of these stones wouldn't cause her harm. Was it this same spirit that protected her a few evenings ago when the crowd with torches and less than pure intent had descended upon Stonehenge? Rather than calling the coven towards the structure, maybe the group were trying to harness the structure's power. The ancestors guarding Stonehenge had forced them away, refusing to allow them to use its magic to cause harm.

The deep cold spirit of the rock led rather than forced Stella towards the space in between worlds. She walked through the shimmering haze.

The Cavern

Stella found herself in a huge underground cavern. Words echoed around her. Incantations from three groups, each gathered around a fire. Stepping backwards, into the shadow of an archway she peered through the haze, which was caused by the fires and not the mystical doorway she had entered.

The rocky dirt floor of the cave, big enough for the three fires and seating for many more people than the fifteen she counted. Leading away from this space were five corridors: hallways leading to other rooms, maybe prisons, or an apothecary.

Quietly sliding down the wall, taking up as little space as possible, Stella closed her eyes, for a second. Images of herself flooded through her senses - touch, taste, sight, smell, and sound. She wasn't called Stella then. Hecate was her name. One of three sisters who ruled this underground coven.

Opening her eyes brought her back to her present situation with a jolt. An old crone, her face a few centimetres from Stella, her putrid smelling breath hissed, "I know you." Stella held her breath, not only to stop the acrid smell permeating her nostrils and her mouth. "You shouldn't be scared," she continued. "You are a leader." As quickly as the crone appeared, she vanished.

Had Stella imagined that encounter? Her hand felt for the cloak around her shoulders. Not her invisibility cloak, but one gifted to her from the spirit of the stones. So far her energy had not caused any issues. No alarms or triggers that she could see.

THE ENCOUNTER WITH the crone had opened a flood gate of memories of her past life, as Hecate.

She stood up and took a couple of steps towards the middle of the room. The jaggedness of her memories brought with them a sense of power. Authority pulsed through her veins. She heard herself command the groups, "Stop!" Fifteen pairs of eyes turned and stared at her. She quelled the beating of her heart, or rather Hecate, who appeared to be inhabiting her body, quietened the noise of her heart that she thought must surely give her away as an imposter.

"Who is in charge?" she demanded of the group who were still staring at her. No one spoke. "Leave!" she commanded. "Except you." She pointed to a woman that Stella recognised from the laundrette; the blonde lady who had hidden the wands.

Fourteen women scattered, disappearing along each of the hallways, without speaking a word. Blondie remained.

Before any words could be uttered an insistent tapping on her arm caused Stella to turn to her right.

"Wake up," whispered a tiny voice. Stella fought her eyelids, a rising panic as she found it difficult.

"Now, Stella." Flix's voice was firm, with a hint of panic. This was a command.

Stella took a deep breath and as she exhaled, she pushed her energy as hard as she could. Thud.

Her eyes open she found herself on the floor of the flat.

"Was that a dream, or something else?"

"Definitely something else. Where were you?" Flix asked, the concern in his voice was unmistakable.

"Stonehenge. Then a large underground cavern. I was me, but I was also someone called Hecate. Is it possible to cross back and forth between lives?" Stella asked.

"It's possible, but only a few magical beings can manage it."

"Flix, why did you call to me? To come back, to wake up. What was happening?" Stella got to her feet. It was difficult to tell what time it was, but she wanted a coffee. She filled the kettle with water from the tap. Flix followed her and sat in the middle of the table. He waited for the kettle to boil before speaking.

"Your aura changed colour. Our aura can change for several reasons, emotions, exercise, illness, stress. Your aura is normally a mix of green and purple. It does change intensity and hues depending on what is happening. When I woke up, your aura was darkening significantly. Black can mean power. It is not necessarily a negative, but your aura was changing so rapidly, the only thing I could think of was to call you back." He eyed the cup in front of Stella. "Is that coffee?"

"Yes, it is. I have no idea what time of the night it is, but I'm awake now," Stella responded.

"What do you know about Hecate and her sisters?" Stella asked the sprite. Images, like scenes from a movie, kept coming. Scenes that weren't making any sense. Stella eyed her cup. She was going to need more coffee.

"Over two hundred years ago, Hecate and her sisters were members of a large coven. Hecate was voted the leader. She was fair and even tempered, and a healer. The sisters were part of one of the oldest magical families in any realm. Over the years there were many arguments amongst the coven as people vied for the leadership."

"Ailsa was a distant cousin of the sisters. When she challenged Hecate to a magical duel, she won, and Hecate and her sisters were exiled. No one knows what happened to them. Once Ailsa was in charge, the coven was never the same again. Many left and formed their own covens. Others stayed. Ailsa spent her whole life in the pursuit of power and strength. She was only happy if she was taking magic and power from others."

"Was it her coven that caused the trouble last year? And the year Luna lost her family, was that Ailsa as well?"

"We could never prove who was the instigator behind those events, but Broomhilda is worried it may be Ailsa that is causing the trouble. If she has cast a spell to cause the illnesses across both realms; that's something Broomhilda needs to know as soon as possible." Flix started pacing back and forth on the table.

"Ailsa won't stop until she gets what she wants. She banished the sisters, and she has stockpiled so much magic already." Stella stood up, stifling a yawn. "I am curious to know if the rest of her coven are as keen as she is, or whether she is coercing them somehow."

"Now that's a good question," Flix said. "It's three o'clock in the morning, do you think you should try to get some more sleep?"

"Probably," Stella answered. "But it's more important we talk to Broomhilda. If we can offer information that will help stop the curse and cure the allergies, then we need to act immediately."

"I can't argue with that," Flix admitted.

Flix hopped into Stella's coat as she shrugged it on over her shoulders.

With a swift swipe of her hand, Stella opened a portal. Right in the middle of the room, a shimmering light the size of a small door appeared between her and the kitchen bench. With her fingers crossed that Brigid's tavern was on the other side, she walked through to whatever was waiting for her.

THE TAVERN WAS CROWDED, but not with the usual revellers. The benches and tables had been pushed to one side and it was set up as a makeshift hospital, with stretcher beds. Maise and Brigid were huddled together behind the bar, talking to Broomhilda.

Stella tapped Brigid on her shoulder. Brigid and Maisie turned at the same instant and the three friends embraced.

"We have news." Stella lifted Flix out of her coat and put him on the bar, so he could see and hear the conversation. Broomhilda landed next to the sprite.

"The short version is that it appears in a past life I was Hecate. Ailsa is behind this curse, the allergies, and most likely other troubles as well. Ailsa's' coven is in a huge underground cavern system somewhere," Stella said, as Brigid handed her a tankard. Taking a sip of the strong coffee reminded her of who she was today. Hecate was a part of her, and maybe she could harness Hecates' knowledge and power to help restore the balance in the realms in this life.

"You have a way of arriving and changing everything." Brigid smiled, referring to another time when Stella had arrived in the middle of the tavern.

"Do you have Hecate's memories?" Broomhilda asked.

"It is like she is part of me but also like I am watching her life as a movie that is playing inside my head. She did try to take over, back in the cavern, but Flix woke me up." Stella stopped to take another tip of the calming dark liquid. For Stella, coffee energised and calmed her, a necessary balance for all she was and who she was becoming. "I think if I tried, I could access her memories and help banish Ailsa."

"That sounds dangerous," Maisie said.

"It will be," Broomhilda agreed. "But if we succeed, we can return these people and all the others, to full health." She pointed to the half dozen patients still on the stretchers in front of them. "Is the apothecary empty?"

"Yes," Brigid replied. "We set up in here so there would always be someone here."

"Are you ready to try to access Hecate's life?" Broomhilda asked Stella.

Placing the tankard back on the bar, Stella looked at her friends. She turned so she could see the people lying on the floor, trying to sleep to give the herbal poultices time to heal their wounds. Some had scratched the afflicted areas so much that they were bleeding. She knew hundreds of people here and back home, were suffering similar fates. Going to sleep and delving into Hecate's life was daunting, but not as unnerving as a future where Ailsa and her coven had taken people's magic and power. Whatever scheme Ailsa was planning, many hundreds of people would suffer. Stella knew that already.

"Brigid, Maisie, I need you to stay here and tend to anyone who comes in seeking help. Maisie, I know you both want to be there, but your skills are best placed here. I will look after Stella, I promise. Flix, you are with me," Broomhilda said.

Stella hoped she sounded braver than she felt, with her legs wobbling like tubs of jelly. "Broomhilda is right, these people need you to stay here. I will be back in no time at all." Stella gave both Brigid and Maisie a look that she hoped relayed *don't you dare cry or hug me, or I'll cry.*

Brigid took hold of Maisie's hand and held it tight. "We'll hold the fort here. Good luck, although you won't need it. We will all meet back here for a tankard of coffee, or something stronger, very soon."

Stella smiled at both her friends. After returning her gaze they turned away, not wanting Stella to see them cry. She bit back tears herself. Her arms felt like ice cream melting in the summer sun. Committing to memory the space where she instantly felt at home, the wooden floors, the carvings on the walls, the metal hooks where the tankards hung at the end of the day. The bar that Brigid's ancestors had carved from an ancient tree, permission being granted from the stewards of the fairy glen.

The heavy wooden door swung open, letting in three more souls, scratching at their arms, sores on their legs oozing blood. Stella followed Broomhilda and Flix out into the night and down the road to her apothecary. This had to work, to heal all those who were suffering. It wasn't their fault there was an evil spirit seeking power and revenge. Her resolve grew stronger, as did her body, with each step she took.

Her *Book of Spells* lay open on the bench in front of them. The last time she saw the book it was in her flat. It lay open at one of the pages in the back that Stella hadn't read before.

Powerful wisdom is created by collecting the magic and knowledge across the ages. This can be donated voluntarily or taken by any means necessary. A word of caution, this spell, once invoked, is nearly impossible to reverse. A pandemic aimed to weaken and confuse, a plague, to disorient and weaken those with the most knowledge and power. Work on fear of contagion. People will isolate, their defences weakened.

The spell has the most power when invoked during the dark moon.

Reversal of this spell is only possible with the aid of the one who controls the elements, the one with the knowledge of the ancients. The one who is marked by the coven of three. To have any hope of reversing the effects of this incantation, the reversal must occur before the first full moon after initial invocation.

Watch out for the mark of the thirteen.

On the opposite page were the words:

The moon casts its magic in phases. These phases repeat every twenty-eight days or so. A cycle that has been the same for as long as anyone remembers and even long past when people began walking on the earth. The phases provide us with an opportunity to plan, work on ideas, release what no longer serves, let go, reflect, and start again. The ebb and flow of the tides and the way plants grow, and flourish are intrinsically linked to this phenomenon. Even if we do nothing and don't believe in the metaphysical power of the moon, it will still weave its magic in our lives.

Stella flipped to the next page, which gave additional information on each of the phases of the moon, the new moon, the waning moon, the full moon and the waxing moon.

"We need to do this now if you are ready. We are running out of time if we want to reverse the spell by the full moon," Broomhilda said, pointing to the stretcher on the floor. "Lie down here and try to relax. Flix and I will weave a protection spell that will keep malevolent beings away but allow Hecate's memories to return. All you have to do is rest and remember."

Stella nodded. She glanced at Flix, who was concentrating on weaving the enchantment around her. She lay down, with her coat wrapped firmly around herself for added security, she rested her hands by her side and closed her eyes.

The Mark of the Thirteen

BROOMHILDA

To say she was feeling frustrated was an understatement. The head of the fairies was searching for a book. "I know it exists! By the heavens I know it exists!" she yelled at the night sky full of stars that illuminated the fairy glen.

She had left Flix by himself to weave the spell of protection around Stella, but she didn't want to leave them alone for long. Too many things could go wrong. Stella was powerful, but she was relatively new to the craft. If indeed she was Hecate in a previous life, that added yet another layer of complexity.

"The book must be here. I have searched everywhere else that I can think of." She lit up the biggest tree in the glen with her wand - over a thousand years old with roots so big they looped up out of the ground and back down again. The branches reached out across most of the glen, home to many species of insects and small animals. Broomhilda dulled her wand, so the light didn't blind any of the creatures who were still awake. "Does anyone here know of the ancients' book? It is leather bound and has all sorts of information the ancients wanted us to know. It was hidden somewhere safe, so that the information was kept from those with evil intent."

An owl, a giant next to Broomhilda, flapped down from one of the upper branches, gently placing a book at her feet. Returning to the top of the tree, the owl flew around the tree before settling on a branch to watch what happened next.

"Thank you!" Broomhilda yelled to the majestic bird.

Stella was in a deep sleep when Broomhilda returned.

"Nothing out of the ordinary yet," Flix reported, the relief in his voice evident. Broomhilda wasn't so sure. According to the book she was holding, if a powerful witch ended up meeting one of the powerful beings from a past life, things could get a little complicated. If Hecate was stronger than Stella - Broomhilda left that thought unfinished, as she prepared the tonic, just in case.

STELLA

As soon as she closed her eyes Stella felt herself dragged back into the past. In a long room a table nearly filled the space, as it stretched from one end to the other. At least thirty people were seated along the benches, with spaces for some thirty more. The remains of a feast, empty tankards, plates with bread rolls, fruits, and vegetables, interspersed with garlands of daisies, marigolds and sunflowers. The Feast of Litha. Mistletoe, elderflower, and lavender hung in bouquets with the lanterns.

Through the open door, was a bonfire, with children dancing and singing and the elder witches with them, teaching them the history and the stories surrounding this celebration. Stella could hear snippets of everyone's conversation, until Hecate spoke, "We are the blessed ones, with our magic and our powers. Others fear us, but we don't need to punish or hurt them. That creates riots and problems that our magic alone won't solve. Magic and non-magic folk can live alongside each other."

Stella felt the mood of the room change. Not everyone seated around the table shared Hecate's views. One of the younger witches seated to her left, stood up and addressed the crowd. "I don't agree with my cousin Hecate," she spat the name as if she had just insulted the woman called Hecate. Stella felt the other part of her fume as the anger built up inside. "We can't be nice and good and accommodating to everyone. Before long it will be expected of us that we fix everything, granting wishes like a genie. *Build me a house. Find me a lover. I want a pony.* Where will it end?"

"Ailsa, sit down." Hecate grew impatient. "I am not suggesting we give people everything they ask for. That would be silly and create even more problems. What I am proposing is that we work with them, to heal illnesses, and stop wars, so they can learn to achieve things for themselves, without the additional stresses. We are still in control of our own magic. We have been given a gift, each of us here, and we should use it wisely."

"I propose we get rid of non-magical folk altogether. Then we can do what we want with our magic. Who agrees with me?" The majority of those sitting around the table raised their hands at Ailsa's question.

"What are you going to do now cousin?" Ailsa sneered at Hecate.

Stella felt the anger and disappointment rise up in Hecate. Two women, Hecate's sisters, joined her, taking her by the arms and leading her outside. They walked in silence until they reached a clearing. The witch on her left, Sinead, waved her arms and a little cottage appeared. The three women crossed the threshold. Sinead waved her arms again and the invisibility cloak descended on the cottage. Stella felt the magic of the three women, the bond they shared.

"We warned you, sister," the younger witch, Tabitha said, none too gently. "But you were too sure of yourself to believe us, or to see it for yourself. Ailsa has a strong following, the *Mark of the Thirteen*, we counted at least twenty-five in that room bearing the tattoo. They will have their way unless someone can stop them."

LUNA

Ten people were lying on make shifts beds in the tavern, holding the poultices on the worst of the red patches on their skin. The relief on their faces spoke a thousand words, but unfortunately, not before some sufferers had scratched their skin raw. Passing out some more cooling ale, infused with chamomile and lavender, Tizzie glanced over at Catherine, who was handing out crusts and stew to those well enough to eat solids. "We need a bigger area and a way of providing the remedy to larger groups of people."

Catherine nodded. "We might be able to use the old Macdonald farmhouse. We would require larger amounts of the herbs. There might be enough growing throughout the region."

"We don't know how far the allergies have spread, and whether it is contained to our realm. Luna, what do you think?" Tizzie called to her friend who was scribbling something in a leather-bound book.

"I think this is old magic, from long ago, and I think it is targeting specific families, old and powerful families." Luna's hands ached, arthritis pinching every joint. Kneading dough for the healing biscuits was hard work for the crone. "I think we should stop trying to do this the hard way, and we should instead use proper magic, the sort of magic the *Mark of the Thirteen* would use, to beat them at their own game."

STELLA

Stella could feel Hecate's anger. Her energy and power building up like steam until it was so full the only option was to blow. Despite her best intentions at doing things the right way, she felt that the only recourse was to use magic against the others in her coven. A dull ache pulsed in her temple as she tried to calm Hecate's power. She was finding it difficult to pick where Hecate stopped, and Stella started.

She felt herself being dragged backwards. She tried to spin around, fearing Ailsa had somehow found the sisters secret cottage, flinging her arms to stop being taken.

"Whoa steady on, you are bigger than us." Stella heard Flix's voice. She fought against Hecate, to open her eyes as Stella. It was like pulling a stick out of thick mud on the riverbed. When she eventually managed to open her eyes, she found herself on the floor of her apothecary, with a fairy and a sprite fluttering above her, a look of concern on each of their faces.

"Is she back?" Flix asked Broomhilda, "Is it Stella, or someone else?"

"I don't know about Hecate, but I'd love a coffee," Stella said in the bravest voice she could manage.

"It's Stella!" Flix grinned. "Welcome back! You had us worried for a while."

"Why? I wasn't gone for long, was I?" Stella wiggled her arms and legs.

"You were gone for a few hours, although time travels differently in a dream state." Broomhilda confirmed. "Maisie has called in twice now to make sure you were okay. Brigid sent a tankard of coffee for when you came back." Stella leapt to her feet, picked up the drink and gulped the cold drink down in a few seconds. Coffee mightn't be the drink of choice yet in seventh century Scotland, but Stella was forever grateful that Brigid made sure she had a supply on hand.

Stella and Hecate

Maisie and Brigid arrived with some food and hot coffee. "Stay on the stretcher until you have eaten some food and I tell you to move. Sudden movements after the dream state you were in could cause problems," Broomhilda said sternly enough that Stella sat back on the bed, after hugging her friends.

"I think we have been looking at the problem the wrong way around," Stella began. "We could continue as we are, and we would eventually cure all the people in our realms that have the virus. The aim is to annoy and distract people, rather than kill anyone. In our realm, after the covid pandemic of 2020, any mention of a pandemic makes people twitchy. It is affecting mainly the middle aged, wealthy, white collar community. Ailsa wants to get rid of those people with no magic and take the magic and power from those who do."

"You said we were looking at this the wrong way," Broomhilda prompted. "What do you suggest?"

"We have been using herbal remedies and traditional medicine. Treating one person at a time. What if we used magic? Powerful magic, that could cure everyone at once?" Stella said, with a wave of her hand. As she did so, she felt her energy surge. The others noticed too, and they ducked out of the way of the light that flew from her fingertips.

"Was that me, or Hecate?" Stella wondered aloud. "I could see myself, or maybe who I was in my former life, waving my arms and healing everyone who was suffering this ailment, banishing the curse forever. Is that even possible?" More alive than she could remember feeling before, every part of her tingled with energy and excitement. She felt taller, and more confident. Should she be worried that her alter ego was taking over?

"Can you remember your life, before you met Brigid and Maisie?" Broomhilda asked.

"My four children and the curse that tore us apart. My childhood, losing my parents, yes it's all still there." Stella paused. "But so are recollections of life with Sinead and Tabitha. It's weird, it's like I am the one person, Hecate and Stella. There's no fighting in my head or anything. I just know things, about spell casting, and using magic, old powerful magic. It's like I've always known this."

Broomhilda opened the book she had located in the fairy glen. "It is rare that someone can assimilate so well with their past lives." She held up the book so that the others could see it. "This is full of tales of witches and wizards who lived hundreds of years ago. Tales of how they used their power to defeat evil. It also outlines some not so positive spell craft, which is why it was hidden years ago, to keep people like Ailsa from using magic for the wrong reasons."

"Do we think Ailsa might have her own copy?" Maisie asked.

"It is more likely that there are many similar books. People are always journaling, writing their spells down, their book of spells or grimoire passed down through generations. It is easier than we might think, for people to get hold of information, if they really want to." Broomhilda said.

"What about Stella's idea?" Brigid asked. "Would it hurt her, if she was to try what she suggested, to fix the issue with her magic, Hecate's magic?"

It was a crazy idea, but the sparks of excitement bouncing around her told Stella that maybe, just maybe she was on the right track. She concentrated on listening to the conversation around her. The power surging within her crackling like an open fire was more than a little distracting.

All eyes were on Broomhilda as she scanned through the *Book of the Ancients*. "The battle between good and evil has always existed. Even more so when we add magic into the equation. People are greedy and hungry for power. The *Mark of the Thirteen* has survived throughout several centuries in one form or another. Hecate, and some of our ancestors before her, did use magic to resolve challenges between covens."

"I sense there is a problem, a price for using magic. Especially that much powerful magic, and if Stella is channelling Hecate's magic too, isn't that dangerous?" Flix asked his boss.

"I honestly don't know." Broomhilda slammed the book shut. The book jumped around a bit, before is disappeared into thin air.

"Fae magic. The book is now safe from falling into the wrong hands," Broomhilda explained. "In terms of whether you can use magic to cure this current illness," she said to Stella, "Yes you probably can. Will using that amount of power injure or impact you, I am not sure. It is up to you, whether you do this, or whether we continue to work on other options for healing."

Stella had lost all track of time. She guessed it was morning sometime. She was likely late for work. Baz would be worried. She had grown fond of Baz, and Mae and their clientele. If she never saw them again, they would always wonder what had happened to Stella, but they would get on with their lives.

Her children were grown up and living their best lives overseas. It tore at her heart, the thought that she might never see them again, never have the chance to reconcile. They would miss her if she disappeared too. At least the younger two would. She glanced at Brigid and Maisie, both trying not to stare at her, or cry. Her friends, her coven, she would miss them nearly as much as she would miss her children.

If she did nothing, then Ailsa would win the battle and take magic and power that didn't belong to her. People would be hurt, or worse. Her head pounded. She knew what she had to do.

"I think I need to be alone for a while." Her voice little more than a whisper. "I want to sit with the options and this power that is mine, or rather ours. Flix can stay and guard me if you like but can everyone else go back to the tavern. I'll come and find you when I'm ready." There was a strength and a certainty to Stella's voice. She heard it and felt it. The others did too.

Brigid and Maisie embraced Stella in the biggest hug. Not a word was uttered. Energy was shared, and the connection shared between the three, was stronger than before. Stella felt it, they were entwined together, no matter the distance, by tiny threads of gold. *Fae magic* a voice in her head told Stella. Hers or Hecate's?

After her coven followed Broomhilda out the door, Flix shut it and sat in front of it, cross legged, weaving a protection spell around the apothecary. Descending on the building like cobwebs, the net of security to protect Stella's travels.

Stella yearned to be sitting in a clearing of a forest with ancient trees and a stream running through the middle. *Visualise*, whispered the voice deep within, an ancient knowledge awakened.

Her fingers tingling with anticipation, as ever so slowly the wooden walls and floor gave away to a soft mossy forest floor. She could hear the trees whispering to her. Tall trees, taller than any building she had seen, reached up into the sky. Her stomach lurched, dizzy as she looked up into the canopy so far above her. Stella wriggled her toes on the forest floor, grounding herself. As she sat on a rock on the edge of the stream, she plunged her feet in. She gasped. The cool water permeated every part of her.

The bird song and the buzzing of the hundreds of insects who also called the forest home created the best soundtrack she had ever heard. Concentrating on the feelings, as each of her senses drank in the peace and tranquillity of the environment, she breathed in the fresh air in the ancient forest. Leaning over the stream Stella splashed cold water on her face. A few drops of water on her tongue. Touch, smell, sight, hearing, and taste. All fed by this forest and the elements contained within its very soul.

After a few minutes marvelling at her situation, she stood up. An enchanted ancient rainforest. In which realm had she travelled to? Was this somewhere that Hecate visited with her sisters? Crossing the clearing, she came to an overgrown path. She followed her intuition or maybe her memory of the past, along the path lined with dog rose bushes, the overgrown thorny variety, the rosehips healing properties. Careful not to catch her leg on the thorns, or trip on the many broken branches that lined the way, the path led Stella deep into the forest. Forest spirits darted about, too quick for Stella to see, other than quick flashes of light as they passed by.

A grey stone cottage with a thatched roof stood a few metres in front. The more steps she took, the further away the cottage appeared to be. She quickened her pace, the cottage felt so familiar, home. Just as she was close enough, she reached out her hands to turn the gnarled doorknob of the wooden door, the building disappeared.

The forest grew dark. Her senses were playing tricks on her now. Was that the sound of an owl or a dragon? Where was the moon? What was that flash of light? She could smell a fire burning, close by. Feeling the familiar surge of energy, the panic rising in her chest, Stella stopped. She closed her eyes and sat down at the base of the closest tree.

I'm here for a reason. The forest must hold a clue or a solution. What would Hecate do? The pounding of her heart, as her life and Hecate's joined, magnified her strength. Stella stood up. Before her brain registered what she was doing, she held out her hands in front of her and yelled "Stop!"

If a pin was to drop, Stella would have heard it. All noise and movement in the forest ceased the second she had commanded it to.

"Show yourself." Barely had the words left her lips than a mirror stood in front of her. Two women in the mirror. Stella recognised herself. The other woman was Hecate. Stella knew this beyond doubt. The two women were holding hands. As Stella watched, the two women became one. Stella was gazing at her own reflection. Suddenly it made sense. She was Stella but armed with the memories of her time as Hecate, she had the wisdom and knowledge to defeat Ailsa.

This was the realm that during her time as Hecate, she had lived in with her sisters and been exiled by Ailsa and her coven. Ailsa's power grew stronger the more people she coerced into following her. She was stronger in the cavern or in the room where she had stolen the coven and sent Hecate away. Stella, and Hecate received their strength from the elements, nature and the ancient world. Here in the forest. Was it that simple?

There didn't need to be a battle. Stella could restore the balance of nature and reverse the effects of the incantation.

Charged with the magic of the elements, boosted by mother nature's power, she looked down at her hands, clenching them open and shut. Stella closed her eyes and with her hands outstretched in front of her walked slowly forward.

Hearing a quiet whisper, *now,* she opened her eyes.

In the middle of the clearing, in the darkness and the silence the forest waited for her command. Holding her hands outstretched, reaching up as high as she could she spoke firmly, *"I call upon the spirits of the ancients, to hear my words."* Stella moved her arms until they were stretched out on either side. *"To heal those afflicted by malevolent magic, they will suffer no more."* Stella pointed her hands and her fingers down towards the forest floor. *"Earth, water, air, and fire keep safe and let no evil befall those in any realm. Restore the balance of power for now and always. So mote it be."*

MAISIE EMBRACED STELLA the second she opened the door and entered the tavern. Brigid handed Stella a steaming hot tankard, "With a nip of something stronger." she winked, grinning broadly.

"What did I miss?" Stella asked. She took a long sip of the delicious liquid, a sense of calmness descended. She was in the tavern with her coven.

"As it happens, quite a lot. Luna worked out the solution to the allergy problem. Not that we need it now, but it is handy to have, just in case. Thanks to Luna and her coven we know the quantity of herbs and oils to soothe and heal the skin. We made as much as we could, ready to administer to everyone who could get here to the tavern. As we no longer need the antidote, we are keeping it in the cool room."

Savouring the taste of the whiskey infused coffee, Stella asked, "So did my spell actually work?"

"It appears so," Broomhilda confirmed.

"What about in Australia?" Stella turned to Flix, as he appeared next to Broomhilda.

"From what I can tell, there are no more instances of the allergies, or the virus anywhere in that realm either," Flix confirmed.

"It is so good to have you home," Maisie said, passing Stella a plate piled high with a combination of sweetmeats and fruit.

Stella looked at Broomhilda, and back to Brigid and Maisie. "I must go back. Just for a little while. I don't think it is finished yet. Ailsa won't just walk away."

Flix nodded. "I agree. I will join you. Before you ask, your children are fine. Fae magic will keep them safe from harm, now and forever. Broomhilda and I saw to that. We are finally learning from the mistakes from the past."

"You will need to be careful when you return. Things may have changed. We don't know how Ailsa will react. We will keep an eye out here for any trouble and Flix will report back any concerns," Broomhilda said.

"I'll be back as soon as I can." Stella promised, giving Maisie and Brigid a hug. You are my coven, and we have spells to cast during the next full moon." Flix hopped into the pocket of her coat as Stella pictured the flat and waved her arm in front of her. A sweeping motion, like she was opening a curtain.

Remedy and Relief

"**I** am so tired." Stella yawned. "Baz must be wondering what happened to me." She pulled open the corner of the curtains, "It's dark outside, was I away for a whole twenty-four hours?"

"You were away a while," Flix conceded. "Broomhilda used fae magic, so we are back in time to before your last trip to Stonehenge. You have six hours to sleep, and Baz won't even know you have been away."

Stella's eyes were closed as soon as her head touched the pillow. Her alarm at five am woke her from the first dreamless sleep in a long time.

"I'm going to have a shower, then some coffee," she told Flix. He gave her the thumbs up signal from his position on the windowsill.

A miracle. The road announcer said of the news that all those suffering from the unknown allergy virus were cured. Not a scar anywhere to confirm that any pandemic had occurred. *The government has confirmed that they have cured all the sufferers through hard work, science and the thoroughness and competence of the medical professionals.*

"I wonder if anyone actually believes this stuff?" Stella said, pouring some milk into her cup.

"People believe what is easy for them, what won't impact their lives." Flix said, joining Stella at the table. "Are you going to talk to Kai this morning?"

"Yes, as soon as I finish this." Stella drained the last of her coffee. "I want to visit Mildred and the laundrette this afternoon. To gauge if there is anything to worry about."

Kai met Stella at the bottom of the steps. She looked like she was about to hug Stella but thought the better of it. "I don't know how you did it, but thank you," she said awkwardly. "I have been released from the coven, no longer stuck doing their bidding. I am free to find my friends and resume my life."

"That's wonderful news, Kai. Will you be returning to your friends straight away?"

"Once I confirm the coven meant it and that my friends won't be in danger if I return." Tears welled in her eyes.

"Do you know where I was taken from?" Stella asked.

Kai nodded.

"Go to the tavern and tell Brigid that I sent you. She has rooms for rent and she's always looking for reliable staff. I'll return there as soon as I can; I'll help you make sure your friends are safe and you can join them." Stella gave the girl a hug.

"STELLA, YOU'RE HERE early," Baz said as Stella handed him a cup of hot chocolate and a toasted sandwich. "Thank you for breakfast."

"You're welcome. I just wanted to thank you for your kindness, friendship, and all you have done for me while I've been here. I might be moving on sooner than I thought."

"It's me who should be thanking you. Your support during the fire and the drama. I wouldn't have coped without you."

"You would, you're stronger than you think. I'll open up while you finish your breakfast." The line for coffee and breakfast was longer than normal. People were excited and cheered by the news that the virus had disappeared as quickly as it had appeared. Everyone was in a good mood.

The hours flew. Mae called in to tell them that their new staff member was able to start earlier than first thought. "We have promised her the flat upstairs, so it's working out perfectly that you have decided to move on sooner than you thought. If you ever decide to come back this way, there will always be a job for you."

"I appreciate your trust and your generosity. I have learnt so much during my time here," Stella told Mae, who insisted that Stella take a proper lunch break for once. Stella took the opportunity to visit Mildred.

The alleyway that had contained Mildred's shop and the other boutique stores wasn't there. Stella thought she had walked up the wrong street. A mechanics and a car yard stood where only hours before she had purchased herbal tea to aide memory. She opened the door to the office of the car dealership that sold second hand bargains.

"Excuse me, I'm looking for a shop that sells crystals and herbs. I'm new to the area and I thought the shop was on this street. Can you please point me in the right direction?" Stella asked the plumpish, middle-aged man with his feet up on the counter, eating a burger.

"You must be lost love. This is the industrial part of town. You will find tyres, radios, trucks and cars, mechanics and cars for sale. All the posh shops are on the other side of the traffic lights. Near the bus station."

Stella thanked the man, leaving him to his burger and chips. What did this mean? Was Mildred one of Ailsa's spies too? Had she tricked Stella? If so, the trick had backfired. Ailsa, and Mildred couldn't have known about Stella's past life. Were the herbs really meant to help Stella remember or was there another intent? She made a note to talk to Broomhilda about that when she returned to the other realm.

KAI SLID INTO THE BOOTH, as Stella was wiping it down from the previous occupant. "The laundrette is gone. The building I mean. It just isn't there anymore."

"Do you mean it is an empty building? Or an empty block of land?"

"Neither. It's like it didn't exist. The second-hand shop is still on one side, the tobacconist on the other side. I don't know whether we should be pleased or concerned." Kai whispered.

"I'm not sure either. I went to visit Mildred at her shop today and the whole area is now an industrial estate. It has been for years, according to one of the car salesmen. I think they've returned to their realm because their enchantment failed. There's no need for them to remain here. Do you want a coffee? My treat," Stella asked.

"A coffee would be great. Thanks." Kai smiled.

EVEN THOUGH KAI HAD warned her, Stella gasped. Standing at the newsagent, she faced the opposite side of the street. The laundrette sat in between the second-hand shop and the tobacconist. Or rather it used to. There was no gap or gaping hole where the laundrette with its mysterious portal had once stood. Nothing to indicate its existence at all.

HECATE'S WISDOM GREW stronger. Whatever malevolence had been causing trouble here was gone. There was no need to stay here anymore. She felt no magic or mischief here.

Stella reached into the pocket of her coat and lifted up the sprite, "I think it's time," Stella told Flix. "Let's go home."

STELLA HAD EXPECTED to arrive in the middle of the dinner crowd. Instead, the tavern was empty of clients. One long table filled with plates of fruit and breads and cakes was laid out in front of her. Luna, Catherine and Tizzie were seated at the table. Maisie was handing out plates as Brigid placed tankards in front of the guests.

"Our guest of honour!" Catherine raised her tankard. The others raised theirs. "To Stella."

"It was a team effort; I didn't do it myself," Stella said, sliding into the seat next to Luna.

"In this case, you do have to take the credit," Broomhilda said from her position at the head of the table. Standing on the table, with a fairy sized tankard in one hand and her want in the other. Your magic has grown significantly stronger in a very short space of time. Ailsa couldn't have known that banishing you would have the exact opposite effect than she was hoping for."

"You are stronger and braver than all of us," Luna said. "I think if I had been sent away, I would have just curled up in a ball and stayed there."

"You would not!" Tizzie and Catherine cried in unison, both having witnessed first-hand, Luna's courage when faced with a similar threat many years ago. Stella had heard the stories.

The elements— earth, air, water and fire, mixed with spirit—add our intention and our belief. Concentration and manifesting, visualising and knowing clearly what we want the result to be.

Not just for saving the world, these tools in our toolkit can be used for the mundane – having a good day, a positive outcome, healing, communication, abundance and prosperity.

This spell casting, done purposely and with awareness, to focus our abilities and our intent. So much of our lives we are like a passenger, with someone else at the wheel, deciding our direction and the destination of our journey. When we take control and take the helm, with intent, concentration and focus, amazing things begin to happen.

The Final Chapter

"The Mark of the Thirteen have retreated. Part of our realm is hidden by a veil. Years ago, ancestors of mine banished the original thirteen, behind that veil, for their behaviour. That coven has always sought to rule this realm and others. They are often the catalyst for the uprising every twenty-seven years, causing the surges of magic we felt last year. Vying to own all the magic in their realm for themselves." Broomhilda paused as a fairy flew into the tavern through the open door and whispered something that only she could hear. She nodded her thanks to the fae, who flew back out as quickly and quietly as she had arrived.

"Kai's magic and yours Stella, are entwined through generations. The lineage is not exactly clear and to unravel it would take more magic, time and patience than I have." Smiling wryly, Broomhilda continued, "Because of this connection and because you worked together to reverse their spell, Kai and the other people the *Mark* had taken as slaves, are all free. The banishment of the *Mark* is reactivated. Behind the veil they have everything they need, enough food and water, crops, industry, and trade to live independently. Trade only occurs with a specific group of families whose charter it is to keep them on the other side of the veil."

"Our contacts have confirmed that everyone who was afflicted with the virus is healed. People have returned home. Everyone is safe," Brigid confirmed. "Once again, thank you Stella for saving our people, our realm, and yours."

"We have a surprise for you," Maisie said excitedly. "You missed the dark moon and the new moon festivals. It is nearly Imbolc. We are planning a celebration to welcome you back and to thank you for everything."

"I can't wait." Stella hugged Maisie and Brigid. "I am so glad to be home and that everyone is safe."

No one saw the figure whose face was pressed against the one window of the tavern. Someone who didn't believe in happily ever after. Someone who would never forgive Hecate. He had plans to disrupt this happy reunion. An Imbolc celebration was just the place to cause mischief. He rubbed his hands together with glee.

Earth, fire, air, water ... and spirit

Full moon, new moon

Hopscotch, skip and jump

Run around, run around, all fall down

A witches most powerful tool is herself and her energy.

Her belief in herself

Her understanding of the natural world and the natural order of things.

Don't be put off or scared by your lack of confidence, lean into it, and remember your magic can move mountains.

The End

Sarah Lewin

If you want to know more about me or my books, here are some details. Alternatively, please make contact via any of the social media listed below:

Email: sarahlewin@sarahlewin.com.au

You Tube: https://youtube.com/@sarahlewinangelwisdom539

Blog: https://sarahlewin.com

Facebook: https://www.facebook.com/SarahLewinAuthor-WitchyMysteryBooks

Instagram: https://www.instagram.com/sarahlewin_author/

Amazon: https://amazon.com/author/sarahlewin

Goodreads: https://www.goodreads.com/author/show/43342156.Sarah_Lewin

Book Bub: https://www.bookbub.com/authors/sarah-lewin

My Witchy Mystery Books:

Witch Wisdom Series:

#1 – Crone Wisdom

#2 – Ancient Wisdom

Spirit Town Cosy Mysteries:

#1 – Autumn Leaves are Falling – available soon

I also have a range of children's books available.

www.ingramcontent.com/pod-product-compliance
Lightning Source LLC
Chambersburg PA
CBHW070614120726
47909CB00004B/1219